THE ULTIMATE PERIL

By
ROBERT ABERNATHY

I0616790

ARMCHAIR FICTION
PO Box 4369, Medford, Oregon 97504

*For more information about Armchair Books and products, visit our
website at…*

www.armchairfiction.com

Or email us at…

armchairfiction@yahoo.

A SECRET WEAPON THAT SPELLED EARTH'S DOOM

Was there even a remote possibility that Earth could be defeated by Venus in an all-out interplanetary war? It seemed unlikely. Venus technology was years behind that of Earth. The massive Earth space fleet was far superior to the copycat fleet of the Venusians. In fact, it seemed that Earth had lulled itself into a planet-wide feeling of over-confidence.

However, there was one man who knew differently. A man who had "escaped" from Venusian captivity. What had the Venusians done to him in those twelve awful days of captivity? Ralph Degnan searched his mind for the answers—but his memory was blank. Could he remember the horrible truth before it was too late…before the destruction of Earth could no longer be avoided?

FOR A SECOND COMPLETE NOVEL, TURN TO PAGE 91

CAST OF CHARACTERS

RALPH DEGNAN
He had been a Venusian captive and they had done something to him—something he must remember in order to save Earth.

MARGARET LUSK
Degnan knew somehow that she played a pivotal role in defeating the Venusian forces—but could she be trusted?

GENERAL FLEMING
It was the toughest decision of his career—to decide whether a loyal serviceman was a patriot, or a traitor to his own planet.

ATHALIE NORTON
An interplanetary war didn't seem to concern her. All she cared about was living for the moment and getting what she wanted.

JAY MARLIN
He was a dedicated military man and probably the only person who might actually believe Degnan's incredible story.

CLARK
He didn't know it, but he was a mind slave to the Venusians; and all he wanted to do was bash in Degnan's skull.

MR. KING
If he allowed Ralph Degnan to meet with Margaret Lusk would it mean the Earth's salvation…or its doom?

CHAPTER ONE

THE *Sheneb* was five thousand tons, built in Venusian yards as a copy, line for line, of an Earth cargo carrier. As such she had served her first few years, driving crewless between Venus and its colonies on the outer worlds.

Now she was converted. Lusterless black, absorbent not only to light but also to far longer wavelengths, hid her magnesium skin, and an atomic blast gun peered threateningly from an airless swivel turret built clumsily into her once clean-cut nose. That was for war.

For her present purpose there were other changes. The cargo decks had been stripped of all equipment and sealed off by partitions from the engine and control rooms forward. That was to protect the Venusian crew from the poisonous oxygen breathed by the prisoners in the hold.

After thirty hours in space, twenty-six under zero acceleration, the cargo decks were uninhabitable. But men, women and children still clung to life there, a tangle of bodies helplessly adrift in the fetid air. The Venusians had provided little ventilation, no light, and no waste disposal mechanism, which last was a peculiar horror in the weightlessness.

But perhaps worst of all was the darkness. It denied them the little comfort of seeing other human faces in their hell. And in the darkness no one could count the living and the dead. And if, floating in that black pit, you bumped against a rigid body, it was not worth the effort to find out whether the stiffness was that of death or the cramped rigidity of space sickness—not the nausea that had wrenched most of the prisoners in the first hours, but the other space sickness that was worse—zero neurosis, free-fall hysteria, any names there are for the primitive terror of falling, falling endlessly into blackness for more than an Earth day now. Very few knew how to take that sensation; many gasped and fought for a support that was not there and lapsed at last into a paralysis of fear.

Not long after acceleration had ceased, the word was passed round that Favreau, Ambassador of All the Nations, was dead. That might mean something in interplanetary politics—but here he was only one of many dead.

A woman's voice, a girl's by the sound of it, was sobbing and talking through sobs, trying to rouse someone named Jim—and failing.

Another voice interrupted her, speaking almost in Ralph Degnan's ear: "Better let him be. If it's zero neurosis, he may be luckier than we are." Degnan recognized the voice as that of the doctor who had tried to calm and help during those first hours of darkness and crushing acceleration and terror. The doctor went on, explaining quietly, as if he were in the clinic, "In that condition blood is drawn away from the brain. It helps combat the derangement of blood pressure in free fall that may bring on cerebral hemorrhage. Zero neurosis may be a survival mechanism."

"Survival?" The girl-voice caught up the word, and laughed with a surprising, bitter energy. "I've been praying for the deflectors to fail when a meteor comes in our path."

The conversation, so close and yet invisible, irritated Ralph Degnan's raw nerves in ways he didn't stop to analyze. He said savagely, "If you've got to pray, who don't you make it for an Earth warship? And dammit, doc—you don't have to be scared to live in free fall."

IN THE silence, Degnan could hear unhurried breathing close beside him. He sensed that the doctor was trying to see him, studying the tones of his voice.

Finally, the steady voice said, "Perhaps you're not afraid, my friend. I'm sure I am, both of *now* and when I try to imagine life in a prison on Neptune... But I think you're upheld by another emotion that has much the same physiological effects as fear. Anger, or hate."

"I'm waiting," said Degnan flatly. "The Venusians never make a mistake—they think. They and their 'total mentality'. I'm waiting."

"There's no chance here."

"Maybe on Neptune, if that *is* where they're taking us."

The girl's voice came out of the blackness, sounding frightened, uncertain. "Who are you? I don't think you're one of us."

"Who's 'us'?"

"Most of the people here," explained the doctor, "are from the colony at Ghrup Shiyap. Attached to the embassy there, as I was. Even when we heard—we hoped we'd have some diplomatic immunity. Maybe we do—they haven't killed us outright."

"I was a clerk in the embassy. I got the job to be with Jim—my brother." The girl's voice shivered. "There wasn't any warning. Only a radio flash—and then they came for us—"

"I believe," said the doctor soberly, "that all the Earth people on Venus were rounded up within an hour of the first news of fighting. The Over Race is efficient."

"They were even more efficient in my case." The others couldn't see Degnan's twisted grin. "They put the finger on me two weeks ago. I didn't know the war had begun until they shoved me on board this ship."

"We don't know much more. It was reported that a Venusian cruiser fired at installations on the Moon, that Callisto was heavily bombarded by Earth ships. No major engagements."

"There will be," said Degnan with grim confidence. "After what they've done, Venus is at war with every country on Earth. That makes the odds in first-class battleships alone better than thirty to their one—and in manpower, if you can call theirs that, still better. We'll smash them."

"I hope you're right," said the doctor, a queer doubtful note in his voice.

The girl asked hesitantly, "Where were you? Before they arrested you, I mean."

"In the Gray Barrens near Ghrup Unur," said Degnan. "Trading with the Under Race... Those are Venusians a man can deal with. Their minds work like ours."

The doctor remarked unemotionally, "Our captors would say that's because we're savages, too."

DEGNAN said nothing. His hatred of the Venusian Over Race was too deep and too precious to waste in words. But the stifled sound that did escape him must have been expressive, for the girl spoke in a new voice, rich with pity: "They must have hurt you terribly. I don't see how anybody could live through two weeks of being their prisoner."

It was like running into something sharp and hard in the enfolding blackness. It jarred the fierce intent anger out of him and left him feeling hollow and weak.

He said shakily, "I don't know. I don't remember what they did to me." His eyes stared into the darkness until he saw points and darts of light that weren't there.

"What's the matter?" inquired the doctor's even voice.

"Twelve days," muttered Degnan hoarsely. "I'm sure of that, anyway. That long between the time they grabbed me and when they put me aboard... But I don't know what happened in those twelve days."

"That's not unusual, you know. Frequently the mind rejects a memory that's too painful."

Degnan didn't answer. He was groping; trying to sound out the frightening abyss that had suddenly opened in his own mind, his own memory.

"Whatever you've forgotten is over and done," the doctor reminded him gently.

Degnan shook his head to clear it, said between his teeth, "Sure. That's right. What matters now is getting out of this, back to Earth—"

He stopped, jolted by the loudness of his own voice. The darkness of the hold had grown suddenly denser with the death-stillness around. The weary murmur of voices, the fainter rustle of movement, had stopped as if everyone had become stone.

And it seemed to Degnan that he had seen a faint light flicker and vanish, but had thought it a trick of his eyes. The next moment he knew it had been real, as a chilly sibilance, like a snake's sound, cut through the silence and came nearer.

He caught an eye-stinging whiff of formaldehyde. There were gasps of hard-held human breath, and the sighing hiss of the propulsion tubes attached to the Venusian's body as it moved purposefully among the helplessly floating, blind Earth people. It could see, no doubt, if only dimly by infrared in the stifling-hot hold.

DEGNAN knew by the stench that the creature was hanging very near him, motionless, for the hissing had ceased. Perhaps it was watching him and no other, with those great sightless-looking eyes whose glittering reflections under light would seem an empty fire of hell...

He almost screamed, and twisted convulsively like a hooked fish—which for all practical purposes he was, for a fang of hot metal had bitten through his shirt and skin at the meeting of shoulder and neck. He felt the barb grate against his collarbone and pain came flooding as he was yanked into motion through the air. Then he was drifting free again— and a hard invisible wall collided violently with him. He scrabbled at it, seeking a hold that would let him launch himself at the enemy he could not see, and the effort thrust him away from the wall to dangle helplessly in the blackness where there was no up, no down, nor any way at all, and he did not know whether the smarting in his eyes was from tears of rage or from the creature's formaldehyde reek.

Someone whimpered like a trapped animal, and Degnan collided again—this time with something soft and moving, another human. They embraced one another by common consent, with the blind need to grasp at a stay in the spinning void. Then Degnan knew that the other was a woman; he felt her strangled sobbing and heard it in his ear, and by that sound was sure it was the girl he had been talking to a few moments ago.

"Steady," he muttered foolishly. "Maybe it won't—"

Something blunt and hard punched him breathtakingly between the shoulder blades, and lights danced before his eyes. Some of the light persisted until he knew it was really there. The Venusian had propelled the two of them, still clinging together, through an opening door into a communication shaft, and there was dim red light in the shaft, enough that Degnan could see and reach out to snatch at the handholds fixed inside it—

He was thrust sickeningly, painfully away. They drifted along the tube toward brighter light, and as their bodies turned slowly in air, Degnan saw the Venusian following. Its hunched leggy form—which, if it had been far, far smaller, scuttling round and round in a kitchen sink, would have been merely disgusting—differed not at all from that of the Under Race, with some of whose members Degnan had talked and traded and almost made friends. But the huge compound eyes, that gave it three hundred and sixty degrees of vision, gleamed with the bale-fires of a dreadful intelligence. Or perhaps you only thought you saw in those eyes what you knew was behind them: the total mentality of the Over Race, which might be called superhuman with as much or as little justice as man's mind could be called supercanine...

It had a long-hafted goad like an elephant man's hook, with which it prodded them impatiently once more. It must be uncomfortable here. The air in the shaft was muggy-hot and stifling with formaldehyde gas, but it was humanly endurable, which meant that the Venusian, save for its breathing apparatus and the complicated protective garment that sheathed most of it, would have died in it almost equally fast from oxygen poisoning and from freezing.

There was something funny—the Venusians had gone to the trouble of exhausting their own air from this part of the ship and replacing it with something like Earth-normal. They must have some very special motive for fishing two living humans out of the hold. Degnan's flesh crawled when he tried to guess the reasons they could have.

THE MONSTER behind thrust them forward again, and they drifted out of the communication shaft into a room—forward of the ship, Degnan judged by its size, and lighted with the murky red glow that was all human eyes could register of what for Venusians was a brilliant illumination.

There were two more Over Beings here, afloat side by side, watching. Degnan knew more about Venusians than most men, but he couldn't read their expressions—his experience among the Under Race didn't help him there;

these creatures were as different in mind from their poor relations as they were in body from man. But he recognized the insignia one of them wore as those of a high officer in the Venusian fleet—surprisingly high to be aboard this miserable cargo shell. Both of them were armed, and Degnan's other thoughts were lost in the craving to get his hands on one of those weapons.

He saw something else that made his heart bound with illogical hope. At four places around the red-lit chamber's periphery the wall bulged smoothly inward, and an air-seal door was inset into each curve. Those, on this model of ship, marked the berths where emergency rockets, provisioned and fueled, were carried when a crew was aboard... And one of those doors was standing open, more red light glowing beyond.

The madness of the idea didn't occur to Degnan then. He twisted and got his first look at the girl he was holding and who held to him. Her face floated before—above, below?—him, ghost-pale in the bloody light, darkly haloed by hair that drifted in wild weightless disorder. As he had half-expected from her terrified rigidity, her eyes were wide, dilated, unseeing. He tried briefly to pry one of her hands loose from his arm, and knew he would have to break her fingers first.

She had to be jarred out of it, and that inside seconds. Already he could hear the hissing of the third Venusian's air-tubes, emerging from the shaft.

Degnan clenched his teeth and slapped the girl's face; her panic grip loosened, and he caught her by the shoulders and shook her till he was afraid her neck would snap. But he saw her lips move, the pupils of her eyes return to normal size, and he whispered sharply, "Do you hear me?"

She nodded dazedly. The Venusian that had brought them out of the hold was hovering close, barbed goad poised; the red chamber was turning slowly about them. Degnan whispered, "There's one chance. When I say 'Go!', we'll shove off in opposite directions. Action and reaction. You try to occupy the one there; I'll take the two on the other side."

She drew a shuddering breath, said, "All right." He was thankful she didn't add what they both knew—that the chance was no chance at all.

"Get ready, then," said Degnan harshly. They braced themselves against each other and waited for their slow rotation to bring them into position...

The high-ranking Venusian floated into Degnan's field of vision with a soft hissing. One of its almost-hands of delicate claws and flattened pads was extended, holding something that gleamed and that Degnan recognized—too late, a fractional instant before it exploded into blinding light.

The flare was literally blinding; when it vanished he could see only confused darkness. He had met it before, when he was seized, and knew it for one of the Over Race's clever new devices for dealing with Earthmen—one harmless to themselves, since it used light invisible to Venusians. But there was something funny about it this time. The darkness didn't stay on and slowly clear up, but he seemed to be plunging into concentrically smaller circles of buzzing nothingness, himself dwindling away to nothing, losing consciousness...

CHAPTER TWO

THE RED light burned once more. The air was murk-red, close and stuffy, and something somewhere was going "Blip...blip. Blip...blip," in a curious paired rhythm.

And someone was shaking him by the shoulders, almost in time to the noises. Degnan snorted, gulped down a sudden sickness, and sat up, looking into the face of the dark-haired girl.

"Turnabout's fair play," he said dizzily, "but you can stop now."

She drew back, gazing at him with intense relief. "Thank heavens! Now maybe you can do something."

Degnan threw his legs over the edge of the bunk he had been lying on and stared blurrily at gleaming dials and instruments set into an opposite wall, very close and curving. He passed a hand across his eyes. "Do—what?"

"Find out where we're going—and—and do something about it."

The man's head was clearing. Now he became aware of the low monotonous rumble of a rocket drive; that, and the cramped quarters, and the red light, told him where they were. But once oriented, he only felt more bewildered. They were in an emergency rocket from the Venusian freighter, and it was under power.

The girl was watching him as if expecting him to produce a rabbit from a nonexistent hat. Her hair, still tangled, hung normally about her face now—one Venus gravity would be the acceleration of the lifeboat—and the traces of hysteria were gone. She was as rumpled and soiled as Degnan; she was thin, and her face with its bright expectant eyes held shadow-smudges of suffering. And for all that she reminded him somehow of Athalie—Athalie far away and dear, a part of the pleasant dream that life on Earth seemed now. But Athalie was blonde and richly curved, and he had never seen her other than immaculately clean, sweet-smelling, well-groomed...

He heaved himself shakily erect, glancing round the interior of the rocket. Half of it was bunks, uncomfortable but endurable for man or Venusian, three of them, one above the other; the other half was filled by an instrument panel with another bunk above that. The blipping came from the panel and went on and on maddeningly.

The controls he saw were odd-shaped, made for Venusian claws, but mostly recognizable; few and simple compared to those of a regular space ship. The rocket was not equipped for complex navigation or sightseeing; there were no vision devices, no calculator.

"That noise," Degnan said over his shoulder, "is a radar echo. This type of boat has an elementary pilot mechanism that automatically heads for the nearest planet-sized body. It's bouncing a beam off the nearest planet—listen." The thing went 'Blip...blip.' The interval is the time it takes for the echo to get back. Twice the distance to the planet in light-time. Which means it's pretty close. If it's Earth, we'd be inside the Moon's orbit."

"If it's— Do you think it's *Earth?*"

"Yes," said Degnan deliberately. "That's the likeliest—considering how long the *Sheneb* accelerated and how long we were in free flight, we could hardly have been close to anything else. It couldn't very well be Mars...and Mercury's beyond the Sun..."

"Earth!" the girl said in a choked voice. She watched him with puzzled eyes as he turned away and sat down heavily on the bunk's edge again. "But—aren't you going to—"

"—do something?" Degnan shrugged ironically. "The robot's steering on the radar-sight, and I couldn't do any better. There should be an automatic parachute-release, too, when we hit atmosphere—but we won't need that. Earth's at war now, and nothing bigger than a pebble could slip past the interceptor barrage. We ought to be picked up before long."

"Oh," sighed the girl.

"Now," said Degnan, "let's you tell *me* something. What happened? How'd we get here?"

She looked at him blankly. "Why—we got away—didn't we?"

"We were about to try. But I didn't duck in time."

"Oh, yes—your plan." She smiled uncertainly, a frown puckering her brows. "Evidently it worked."

"I don't know what you're talking about," said Degnan rudely. "We both must have passed out."

HE THOUGHT hard, aching head in his hands. And cloudy pictures rose in his brain—memories, or half-memories, plucked with difficulty out of emptiness. Himself, wresting the steel-tipped goad from the Venusian's grip—battering at the others with it, smashing a chitinous head. A couple of jointed legs afloat in the air and twitching gruesomely. Thrusting the girl through the open door, diving after her. Launching the lifeboat into space…

In clipped syllables he imparted those fragments to the girl as they occurred to him, and she nodded thoughtfully. "Yes. Yes, that's the way it was."

Degnan flexed his right arm and tested the muscles of his back likewise. He said, "I'm stiff and sore enough to have been in a fight. And if we both remember it, it must be so. But neither of us remembers very clearly—isn't that right? In other words, something smells!"

"You know what the doctor said about memories."

"Uh-huh. We forget unpleasant things." Degnan smiled grimly. "But if I really smashed up three Over Racers—that's a pleasure I'd never forget. And I'd feel good now—but I don't. That bothers me, too." The girl gazed at him helplessly. Degnan grinned with sudden abandon. "The answer I can think of—I must be a dual personality, and one of me's a superman. That's the only way we could have got away like that; we didn't have the chance of a snowball in hell."

He got restlessly to his feet, paced the cramped space of the rocket's cabin. His last sharp-etched memory was of that greater red-lit chamber aboard the *Sheneb*, the watching monsters, the blinding light. Beyond that everything was fuzzy, even now that they had compared notes. And something else was eluding him. Something was wrong about here and now, about this ship.

He turned sharply on the girl. "Look—what are we breathing here?"

She stared wide-eyed and said without conviction, "Air."

"Obviously. But where's it coming from?"

"The aerator. I knew enough to check that, before you came to."

"Yeah, sure," said Degnan softly. "But that's a Venusian aerator. It should be turning out formaldehyde—not oxygen. Furthermore, the temperature here's about thirty degrees Centigrade, where a Venusian thermostat should be holding it at a hundred."

She bit her lip. "Then—the Venusians must have fixed it that way. On purpose."

Degnan looked at her with a surprised new respect. "Go on," he urged. "Develop that thought."

"I—can't," she faltered. "I don't see *why!*"

"Neither do I," said Degnan blackly, and resumed his pacing. "But so help me, I'm going to."

The girl gazed at him with veiled intentness. She saw a rough-hewn face masked now by two weeks' growth of crisp black beard—that must have got its swarthiness from an admixture of American Indian blood, whence also high cheekbones, and a thin, determined mouth that might under the wrong conditions be cruel. It was not the face of a man accustomed to being baffled long.

"Yes," she murmured, "I think you will."

IT WAS less than an hour later when the radarscope changed its note abruptly and emitted sharp staccato sounds that, translated from interplanetary code, were a peremptory "Heave to!"

Degnan had made a note of the rocket control; he shut the power off and, floating weightless once more, sought for and found a two-way radio. He tuned it, and brought in a hard-boiled voice, speaking English with a Latin accent, which said it was the Chilean battle cruiser *O'Higgins,* and ordered, "No funny tricks. You are covered, *senores cucarachas!*"

With fervent persuasiveness, Degnan explained that they were not cockroaches, they were human. The voice sounded unconvinced, then half-convinced—all the same, a booby-trap expert must board them before they could be picked up by the cruiser.

"That," Degnan admitted, "is a sound idea."

The girl caught her breath. "Do you think this ship is a trap with us for bait? That would explain—"

"If in a few minutes we get blown to atoms," said Degnan levelly, "it'll just about explain everything."

But after some fifteen minutes the lifeboat, pronounced safe as inspection could make it, was engulfed by a huge lading lock in the cruiser's side.

Aboard the *O'Higgins* there was gravity again—naturally, since the cruiser had, like all modern warships and very few other vessels, a full gravitic drive, which meant that its acceleration was limited not by human capacity to endure but by its power plant's ability to give out, and that it could spiral faster than an ordinary ship could travel a straight line.

Degnan, bedraggled, unshaven and red-eyed, clambered out of the lifeboat's airlock and confronted a brown smooth-faced little man immaculately glittering in uniform.

"I am Menendez, *capitan de la Armada del Espacio.* And who are you, who come to us under circumstances so peculiar?"

"Ralph Degnan's my name; better make a note of it," said Degnan curtly. "The two of us have just left the custody of our friends the cockroaches; we couldn't be choosy about the circumstances. Ex-freighter *Sheneb*, apparently heading toward Neptune..." He glanced sidelong at the girl; she looked ready to faint now that rescue was an accomplished fact, and was making futile absent-minded efforts to repair her face and costume, without seeming to pay attention to what was being said. Nevertheless, he switched to Spanish, becoming more polite in obedience to the form of the language: "If Your Honor pleases, I will request that he land me at the city of Los Angeles."

Captain Menendez raised a startled eyebrow. He said stiffly, "We land at Valparaiso, six days from now."

"Es preciso." Degnan's eyes bored steadily into the other's. "If Your Honor will check my identity with North American Military Intelligence..."

The captain was startled again, with the other eyebrow. He recovered himself. "Very well. By all means, *senor* Degnan. And while the check is being made, with what may I serve..."

"Un bano!" said Degnan prayerfully.

A BATH and shave achieved in the cramped facilities of a cabin in officers' quarters, and the food he was brought devoured, Degnan lit the first luxurious cigarette in two weeks and thought briefly of the dark-haired girl—mostly of how little he knew about her. He didn't know who or what she was—or even whether that was important.

What was important—a gnawing feeling told him—was the confusion in his own memory. The enemy had done that, somehow; on Venus, Degnan knew, psychology was the mother of sciences, like physics on Earth, and they had had plenty of chance to study the human mind, which they considered so inferior to their own.

It was so vivid, that glimpse of a Venusian like a smashed bug sprawling in midair, a couple of detached legs jerking. Vivid, but somehow it lacked the essential stuff of reality. It fed without appeasing his bitter hatred of the Over Race.

He couldn't say just why he hated them so intensely. It was a feeling scarcely connected with what he, personally, had suffered; the best reason he could think of was his instinctive sense of their abnormality, some monstrousness about them wholly apart from their unhuman form. In a sense, the dominant species of Venus was an artificial product; they didn't came normally from eggs like the Under Race, but out of the hot spawning beds where forcing and selection kept the recessive mutation that had created them alive.

Degnan shook his head angrily. The Venusians couldn't have made him a tool in any fantastic scheme they might have for getting behind Earth's defenses. That left the lifeboat—which some time ago had been cast off into space, headed back toward Venus with jammed controls. And the girl: was she Number One? She looked like only an unhappy young woman who had been an inconspicuous clerk until caught in the vortex of interplanetary war, who was as innocent as her story…which could be checked easily, of course.

He wouldn't have to worry about her any more. Unless—which was unlikely—they ordered him to when he reported in Los Angeles. He lit a second—or was it a third?—cigarette, and tried to let the smoke sooth away his trick memories and the all-too-real recollection of the black and crimson hell on the *Sheneb*.

A knock at the cabin door, and an orderly was there, saying respectfully: *"El capitan le atiende."*

Captain Menendez was affable. "It is impossible for the *O'Higgins* to leave her patrol, Colonel Degnan—but a North

American liaison vessel will come along side to take you off and to Los Angeles. That will be before very many minutes now. Your Intelligence was delighted to hear that one of their agents had escaped the claws of the Venusians. *Y es verdaderamente un milagro, no?*"

"A miracle—yes," admitted Degnan with gloomy reserve. That was just what was bothering him so much.

Menendez looked puzzled; he said severely, "You are more lucky than you know. I have received a dispatch about the ship that you escaped from—a freighter, was it not, of a type like our M3s?" Degnan nodded.

"Then it can be no other. It tried to run away, and the warship that had ordered it to stop was forced to open fire."

"And the people—the Earth people on it?" asked Degnan with stiff lips.

The captain shrugged. "Of course their presence was not known," he said apologetically, then brightened: "But you see how effective is the Patrol. If the *cucarachas* come close enough to look at our Earth—one pounce and we are on them!" He glanced round him, swelling a little, and Degnan sensed the little man's proud confidence in the steel length and strength of his great ship, its power and its armaments that could lay waste to a whole planet's surface. The Venusians too had ships like this, but not as many as the United Nations of Earth; and in the tremendous battleships, compared to which a mere cruiser was a mosquito, they were hopelessly outnumbered.

"Tell me," said Degnan, "how has the war gone? Where I've been, there wasn't any news."

Menendez shrugged again. "Nor have we heard much. In the last days our forces have occupied Neptune and the Venusian moons of Jupiter and Saturn, but that was a trifling affair; they had been evacuated already. So far we are defensive; we guard ourselves and prepare. Of course," he tried to look knowing. "I cannot tell you the plans of the Combined Fleets. But one thing I tell you: this war will not be long."

"I hope you're right," said Degnan, then realized that he was repeating the doubtful words of the doctor on the *Sheneb*.

"Oh, yes—one more business. Do you wish that the *senorita* be sent to Earth with you? She is of your nation."

With an effort, Degnan brought his attention back to that problem. "She'll have questions to answer, I think—" He stopped short. "Yes, send her along."

CHAPTER THREE

ON THE SHORT trip to Earth, Degnan scarcely noticed the girl or anyone else; he was greedily wrapped up in studying a Los Angeles newspaper, borrowed from the lieutenant in command of the courier vessel.

He was somehow disappointed by his first real glimpse of Earth's reaction to the interplanetary war that was only nine days old. There were many columns of "war news" but very little news. A feature article on the interceptor barrage that made Earth a fortress, and which was claimed—it seemed to Degnan not very convincingly—to be far superior to that with which Venus had surrounded itself. On the front page—in boldface type—was a noncommittal communiqué from the new Combined Fleet Headquarters, somewhere on Earth. Elsewhere were articles that hinted nebulously at the plans for a tremendous offensive being perfected by the world's best military and scientific brains at that hidden base, whose location was secret lest the enemy concentrate some desperate, all-out thrust on it.

Degnan snorted, smelling a rat. He knew that there was no need to figure out an attack strategy now; the plans for offensive action against Venus under all conceivable circumstances had been ready and on file for years as a matter of simple precaution, ready to be put into effect at any moment.

Still scanning the paper, he did not notice that his messenger-boat had landed until a crewman touched his shoulder. As he rose, he saw that the port was already open and the girl had disappeared. It struck him suddenly that he had never learned her name; he scowled and told himself to forget it.

It was a sunny afternoon and the sky of Earth was blue. Outside Los Angeles Spaceport he halted on the sidewalk and blinked, almost overwhelmed by the actuality of swarming human life that went on under the shadow of Venusian war.

Gleaming traffic flowed swiftly by, with Los Angeles traffic's traditional disregard for life and limb. The people who crowded the streets in the sunlight wore holiday faces, filled with social gaiety or smug relaxation or petty clinging worries. Among them, the frequency of uniforms, soldiers and spacemen, showed that times were something more or less than normal. But not one of them looked toward the sky in either fear or defiance.

Beside the gateway was a poster, displaying a hideous and inaccurate painting of a Venusian, its prehensile paws upraised in an unnatural pouncing pose. The caption was screamingly funny. It said:

EXTERMINATORS WANTED. ENLIST TODAY!

Degnan stared at it with a curious sense of distaste. There was such a vast difference between this cartoon bogey and the reality of forty million living monsters on Venus who planned and worked coolly, purposefully, with all the power of their alien minds, to shatter and end the carefree world of man...

A MAN WAS standing at his elbow, thoughtfully watching him. Degnan turned deliberately, a chill question ready in his eyes; but that evaporated as he met a familiar face. "Jay Marlin!"

The other grinned easily. "That's right. They told me to shepherd the stray lamb back to headquarters. You look like you need an escort, too—sort of lost."

Degnan nodded slowly, fumbling for words. "I feel like a stranger here somehow. I must have expected...oh, hell, I don't know."

Jay's smile grew quizzically sympathetic. "You must have been through the mill, Ralph. But that's why General Fleming is so anxious to see you. You're the only man who was on Venus when the war began and who got back to tell us about it."

A plain, maroon sedan was waiting. Degnan sank into its cushions with a sigh of disbelief.

He said lamely, "I've not had time to get a report ready."

"You're to make it verbally to the General himself. I told you he was anxious."

Degnan was silent. It came to him like a dash of ice water that he could report exactly nothing on the period of time they would be most interested in. Did he detect, lurking behind Jay Marlin's unchanged friendliness, just the faintest note of watchful distrust? They would be justified in holding him in suspicion. He was forced to suspect himself, too, so long as that torturing twelve-day blank defied him and held its secrets. His hands clenched involuntarily and the blood pounded in his ears with the effort to remember.

"Sorry," he said absently. "What'd you say?"

"I said," repeated Jay, "we're there."

THE LEATHER-BROWN face of General Fleming, district chief of NAMI, was covered by a crossing, branching and interlacing system of deep wrinkles, which, as the shrewd mind behind them chose, could be amiable, stern, persuasive, ferocious, or impenetrable. The General wore his impenetrable look as he listened to Ralph Degnan's tale.

At last he said, "Is that all?"

"All I can remember," said Degnan steadily. "As I indicated—it's quite possible I've forgotten something important."

"Um, yes." The General switched off the recording machine that had been humming quietly on his desk, thus making the rest of the conversation private. "We'll come back to that." He leaned back with half-shut eyes that still watched Degnan narrowly. "The first part of your report, on the Venusian primitives, may come in handy eventually, but hardly now. Your findings are negative; we'd accomplish nothing by trying to stir up the Under Race against its masters, since it's too backward technologically to count at all in a modern war."

"Still," said Degnan, "they're people—in spite of their looks. The Over Race aren't."

The General gazed at him soberly. "To be perfectly frank, Colonel—in your expressed judgment of the Over Race I seem to hear a note of hysteria."

Degnan choked back quick resentment. He said in a carefully controlled voice, "I think we're underestimating them. I'm not a defeatist. But their conviction of their own superiority—"

The General snorted, his wrinkles ferociously. "That's what I mean. You seem to have let them get your goat, to convince you they can defeat us with occult mental powers, or some such rot."

"Remember," said Degnan stonily, "they have total mentality. They think consciously, logically, with their entire brains, while we use only a small part of ours for that, and the rest is unconscious mind—emotional, rather than logical. That's why I think the fact that the Venusians deliberately began this war is...well...ominous. They're constitutionally incapable of fighting just because they're mad. They don't get mad. They've begun it because they think they can win. We outclass them in all ways of making war that we know about. So—they must be ready to make war in ways that we've never heard of." Degnan drew a deep breath, curiously relieved at having brought his own buried fears into the open in plain language.

"They haven't shown much sign of it so far. No Venusians ships, except the tub you were on, have come near our patrols for several days now. They've sent across a good many bombardment rockets—cheap imitations of ours, like their ships—but not a one has gotten through. Now, where's their terrible secret weapon?"

"I don't know. I do have an idea, though, about one thing they must be banking on. Our fleets were prepared long ago; why haven't they already blasted Venus?" The General was silent, and Degnan knew he had touched a live spot. "Maybe it's because our fleets are national, and each of our sovereign 'United' Nations is holding back, for fear of losing its one or two or three battleships and being at the mercy of its Earthly neighbors when Venus is licked."

THE GENERAL squinted at him, observed him in a dangerously soft tone, "You're talking now, Colonel Degnan, about things that are out of your province and mine as well. Strategy is made by Combined Fleet Headquarters."

"I'm on the outside, but I can still think."

"Maybe," said the General with an odd grimness. He made his wrinkled visage stern. "Now I'll tell _you_ about the Venusians' secret weapon. Though I shouldn't have to; you seem to be a casualty already."

Degnan merely stared at him. A moment before he had been hot with conviction; now he was cold, feeling fear contract about his heart again.

"We know what they've been trying to do," rasped Fleming, "and we're putting a stop to it. During the last twenty years, a lot of Terrestrials have been on Venus for shorter or longer periods. And off and on, especially in the last few years, we've been considerably irritated by their kidnapping our citizens—as you were kidnapped. Always the same pattern—grab one of our people, then release him after a while, with apologies but no explanations. And they must have gotten to a lot of other humans without our ever knowing it.

"Now we know their aim was to work on the minds of as many Terrestrials as they could, which was probably several hundred. They're good at psychology and that sort of thing, including hypnosis; I'll grant they know more about that than we do. And they were using hypnosis to turn those people into traitors—so many Venusian agents—back here on Earth…"

Degnan said, fighting against a wild sinking feeling, "You can't hypnotize a man into betraying what he believes."

"So the psychologists tell me," admitted the General heavily. "I'm not saying your loyalty's been subverted, Degnan. But they did get to a lot of people who weren't very well-balanced to begin with. We've been rounding them up—everybody who's ever been on Venus gets checked and double-checked. And we've uncovered a lot of bad eggs already. They've even got an organization of sorts, centering right here in Los Angeles, since most of the ships went out to Venus from here. That's one reason you were given an escort from the field.

"In your case—you can see we'll have to suspend you from active duty. You'll be given an association-test before

27

you leave this building; if its results are negative, you'll be at liberty, but you'll have to come back for detailed psychiatric examination and treatment if indicated."

Degnan was pale under the swarthy complexion that not even sunless Venus had been able to blanch. He moistened his lips, said numbly, "I see."

The General rose and extended his hand. "I'm glad you understand that we can't take any chances. No hard feelings, then?"

"No, sir," muttered Degnan, not knowing whether he lied or not.

CHAPTER FOUR

HE WASN'T surprised when they let him leave after the association-test; he knew enough about such things to be sure that his unhesitating responses had been the right ones. Loyalty to one's nation is evinced by the right automatic responses to certain key words, such as "liberty", "king", "fatherland", "the proletariat"; and loyalty to the species, though a deeper, truer, more instinctive thing can be measured in the same manner.

Whatever the Venusians had done to his mind—and they had obviously done something—hadn't affected his innermost self. They might have blanked out some of his memories and left him with post-hypnotic suggestion to remember things that had never happened, but they couldn't have indoctrinated him.

As he paused undecidedly in front of the NAMI building, a girl's cool voice called, "Ralph!"

He looked up, and saw a vision of splendor—a smooth new sky-blue car, plastic top pushed back, parked by the curb in front of him, and Athalie Norton gazing at him from behind the wheel, a shadow of annoyance on her flower-pretty face that was framed by spun-gold hair.

"What's the matter, Ralph?" she asked crisply. "Did General Fleming deafen you? Get in—you can explain on the way out to the house."

He slid in mechanically beside her, without answering, which didn't seem to bother her. She fed power to the gravity-thrust motor and shot the car expertly out into the traffic stream with a surge that would have spun the wheels of anything whose power was transmitted through wheels. Degnan watched her, reflecting that Athalie did everything like that—surely, with a sort of determined violence. Her fragile blonde beauty was deceptive; behind that mask she always knew what she wanted and got it. Once upon a time she had decided she wanted Ralph Degnan.

"How," he asked, "did you know where I was?"

Athalie smiled secretly. "I have ways—or father has."

Naturally, thought Degnan. Athalie's father was a big man, with the bigness of the corporation he controlled. North American Steel. One way or another, he had made an astronomical amount of money. And Athalie was her father's money's child.

He wasn't sure he was pleased to see her so soon. There were things he needed to work out alone.

"What did they want you for in such a hurry?"

"They wanted," said Degnan grimly, "to tell me I was canned."

She gave him a flashing sidelong glance. "How come?"

"As a psycho, practically. Since the Venusians picked me up, my memory has holes and kinks in it—so NAMI can't trust me any more."

The girl sighed lightly. "Well...that's good. You need a vacation after all those ghastly experiences. Poor Ralph! You can stay at our place and take a good long rest."

DEGNAN was startled by her reaction; then he remembered that his job had never meant anything to her but a minor irritation once its illusion of glamour had worn thin for her. She would gladly have made a kept husband of him; he had sworn fiercely, privately, that she never would.

"Actually," he said carefully, "I'm suspended, indefinitely. That means until the war's over. But...I've got a nasty feeling there may not be any world after this war, Athalie."

She frowned daintily. "You talk like Father. Since the war started he's gone crazy—acts like he thought he was twenty years younger, only he isn't. They requisitioned the *Azor* a week ago; so he offered to remodel it with his own money. And every time I go by our landing field, I have to see what they're doing to it—as if they couldn't fight the Venusians without spoiling that beautiful ship! I'm sick of hearing about the war. If you can't talk about anything else, Ralph darling, please shut up."

"Okay," said Degnan.

She looked at him longer this time, arching a delicate brow, and almost sideswiped a slower vehicle. "Have I offended you? I don't want to..." She had taken the roadway through Elysian Park, and now she turned the power switch to "braking" and let the car roll to a stop on a small branching driveway behind a shielding screen of trees. Then she leaned back against the cushions and her brisk willful self-confidence seemed gone; she was suddenly younger, softer. She nearly whispered, "It's been so long..."

Degnan wouldn't have been human if he could have disregarded that unveiled invitation.

But when she murmured dreamily, close to his ear, "This is real, Ralph. The real thing, and all the rest, all your silly worrying and fretting—cobwebs—" the soft words stabbed him like poisoned knives, and he drew away from her, with eyes grown suddenly cold and remote.

"I don't know, Athalie. I don't know whether you're as real as some of the things I've seen."

"What *are* you talking about?"

He tried to tell her, then, about the prison ship *Sheneb*, the triumphant monsters and the humans whose black nightmare there had ended mercifully in a burst of atomic flame. She listened, uncomprehending, her nose wrinkling at last in disgust.

"That's all over. You're safe on Earth. Why not forget it?"

"I've forgotten too much already, I think. And I've got a feeling that remembering is important not just to me but to a lot of other people as well."

The scarlet pout of her lips was childish, but her eyes were a scornful woman's. "You think Earth won't defeat Venus without *your* help? I thought they told you your help wasn't wanted."

That stung; he snapped, "Nothing matters to you but your own selfishness, does it?"

He'd forgotten Athalie had a temper too. "You're the selfish one! You'd sacrifice me to some crackpot idea! Go on, spout about your patriotism or whatever it is you love more than you do me!" Once started, she didn't give him time for breath, let alone interruption, and her rage was self-fueling. "I hate you! Get out! Out of my car and out of my sight!"

Degnan had grown cooler as she grew furious. "All right," he said quietly. "I'm going."

BEFORE he was out the door, Athalie started the car with a jerk that all but sent him sprawling in the grass. He recovered his balance and watched the sky-blue machine

31

whip out of sight beyond a tree-masked curve, as if racing to a date with a smashup.

Degnan shook his head ruefully and turned away, back toward the main road and the border of the park.

This wasn't their first quarrel, but he had a strong feeling that it might be the last. It was too bad about Athalie, because it really wasn't her fault. She hadn't changed; but Degnan knew objectively that he had, since thirty hours aboard the *Sheneb* and since twelve days of—what?—on Venus.

The blank was still there. It must be that out of it crept the uncanny sense of urgency that was stronger and stronger upon him. Of catastrophe, vast and formless, impending unless—or if—he, and no one else, did something he couldn't quite remember.

As he plodded along the roadside, the scene with Athalie retreated to the back of his mind. Nevertheless, when a car eased to a stop beside him, he thought for a moment she had come back.

Then he saw that this car was different. An older model, black, ill kept, its top almost opaque with dirt and scratches. It had the distinctive personality that old cars acquire, and it was somehow familiar.

But its driver was nobody Degnan had seen before. An older man, his face marked by hard living like his machine's finish, he leaned toward Degnan, thumb still on the button that had opened the door. "Going downtown? Climb in and save your feet."

DEGNAN got in, muttering thanks. As the car rolled leisurely ahead down the curving parkway, his brain clicked with sudden, belated recognition. This same battered machine had been behind them all the way out here, following with a closeness and tenacity that could hardly have been accidental—that obviously hadn't been.

He didn't feel alarmed, but he did know a lively curiosity. He tensed invisibly, waiting for the move that must come.

"Ever been on Venus, pal?"

Ah-ha, said Degnan to himself, and aloud, "You're psychic, huh?"

"Nah," said the driver. "You just got the look. I was there once, myself."

Check, thought Degnan.

"Yeah," said the other man, "I was a spaceman once, believe it or not. Back before gravities, too, when you sweat out most of every trip in free fall. I been to Venus and Mars and all them places out there. Advancing the cause of Man's Glorious Empire—you know. Now I'm retired, on a pension a bedbug couldn't live on." He spat sidewise, out the window. "A guy gets a raw deal when they got no more use for him. Maybe you know something about that, yourself."

"I'm thinking." said Degnan coldly, "that you know more about me than you're letting on."

The man laughed shortly. "Okay. So you know all about me, and I know all about you, Mr. Degnan. Why not? We're two of a kind." Getting no answer, he went on rapidly, "We've got a lousy deal, and we know the system's rotten. Don't we? It all looks fine—" He gestured jerkily out the windows. They were back on a business street now, where even under the sinking sun the storefronts, the glittering beetle-cars, the walking people were luminous with life and color. "All pretty things and fun—but underneath it's rotten, shot full of holes. People, crawling all over the world—there's too many of them, and they're stupid. *We* know it can't last. Don't we?"

"You mean Venus is going to win the war?"

The other flashed a scared, uncertain glance at him. Crawling though the car now was the man's tenseness as the vehicle made its way through the traffic. His driving began to make Degnan nervous. "What do you think?" the man asked.

"I'm no prophet. But I know this," said Degnan bluntly, "that you're human—but the thing that's talking out of you has bug eyes and claws for hands, and breathes formaldehyde."

He saw the man's hands cramp on the wheel; a moment later, as if in instinctive flight, they swerved the car into a sheltering side street. The voice held a hysterical note that was a fusion of pleading and threat: "I'm giving it to you straight. You're one of us. They got part of you, too, back there. They'll never give it back, that part of us, until they win. So they've got to win!" The last words were a whine of fear.

Degnan ruthlessly suppressed the jelly-like quivering of a kindred fear inside him, and sank his voice to an icy tone of menace. "All right, I've heard enough. I'm an Intelligence agent, mister. Drive to NAMI headquarters. Don't try anything; I've got a gun."

That was a bad bluff, he realized as the other snapped on the brake, jerking them forward, and twisted, reaching, and snarling, "The hell you have!"

DEGNAN lunged across the seat; one flat hand caught the fellow under the chin and slammed his head back against the plastic cowl, the other chopped down with split-second timing on his wrist. Degnan scooped the pistol up and leveled it.

"Least ways, I've got a gun now," he amended with a tight grin. He felt almost grateful to the Venusians' slave for providing a splurge of violence to snap him out of his fruitless mental grubbings. And a new idea had struck him;

he added, "But I don't know whether it's really worth while running you in. The likes of you will never damage the war effort much... Tell you what, rat. I'll turn you loose, if you explain about that last line you were handing me."

"What—line?" the man muttered dizzily.

"About the Venusians keeping part of you."

The other tried to look defiantly jeering. "It's not just me. It's you too. They've got your soul on Venus, and you'll never get it back unless you help them win!"

Degnan hesitated, then decided against further questioning. This bird evidently knew nothing, apart from what the Over Race for their own purposes had planted inside his skull.

He pronged open the door and thrust his hand with the gun into a pocket. "Okay, brother—you can go tell the other zombies to scratch my name off their list."

He gazed after the swiftly receding car with a grim smile. That injunction wouldn't be obeyed, he was sure—if he didn't meet that one again, there would be more of the same kind looking for him. Which meant, he hoped, a chance to learn more about the thing that most vitally interested him now.

Without much difficulty, he got his bearings and caught a bus for a part of town he knew well, close to the Municipal Spaceport. His plans were simple: he'd rent a room—since he had to stay in Los Angeles anyway, waiting for instructions from headquarters—lie low, and wait for trouble to come to him.

En route, he went over what he'd learned. It wasn't much. General Fleming had been right; there were Venusian agents, human ones, on Earth. And Degnan knew the outlines of one type of induced delusion that the Over Race used to bend minds to their will.

But what had they used on him?

The business of captive souls, he snorted at. But the fact remained that he had lost, if not his soul, twelve days on Venus... Perhaps a psychiatrist would he able to straighten the tangled threads and ravel out his memories, when they got around to his case. But he sensed unreasoningly that something was going to happen before then, something terrible and irreversible, something that he alone must prevent...

CHAPTER FIVE

IT WAS almost midnight when he finally found a lodging, for the city was overcrowded with the soldiers of the Fleet. The streets were full of them too, even at that late hour, wandering in groups and with girls, carefree as boys on an outing. Earth had known no war in their memory or in their fathers', and their brief military training had given them scant sense of what it might mean.

Degnan went to bed in a fog of depression compounded of his sense of impending disaster, memory of the quarrel with Athalie, and sheer physical weariness.

When he woke at two p.m. the last cause, at least, had been removed, and he felt more equal to the struggle—if only he knew what he was struggling against.

As he ate afternoon breakfast in a second-rate, uniform-packed restaurant, his attention was snared by the modulated tones of a news commentator, rolling from the place's wide-open radio:

"Monitors on the Moon report that Radio Venus has broadcast something like an ultimatum to Earth. Receivers here didn't pick it up, of course, because of the all-wave scrambling by our defense barrage. But I'm authorized to pass on some of the juicier parts; they may give you a laugh, particularly when you remember the news we got a few hours ago—about how the *Gharukh,* the one first-class battleship Venus had under the Armament Limitation Treaty, was caught off base and blasted out of space by the North American battleship *Alaska* and the Chinese *Yang Tse.*

"But now the high spots of the Venusian pronunciamento. The Over Race announces as its war aims the extermination of humanity and conversion of Earth, according to a prepared 'planetary engineering blueprint', into a Venus-type world, with a cloud blanket and formaldehyde-carbon-dioxide atmosphere.

"The alternative to unconditional surrender—destruction by a mysterious 'final weapon', which is ready to strike at any moment, but which the Venusians hesitate to use, they explain, because it might damage the planet Earth itself and put difficulties in the way of their conversion plan. So they call on us to surrender, offering as bait the promise that a 'chosen few' of the human race will be spared and allowed to migrate to Mars—a suitable home for the cold-blooded poison-breathers who now inhabit Earth.

"Surely no more evidence is needed that the war lords of Venus are completely out of touch with reality…"

Somebody in the cafe did laugh at that crack. But Degnan sat staring at the radio, and the glitter of its chromium recalled the gleam of great inhuman eyes, alive with intelligence and a coolly, calculating consciousness of power.

Disgust crystallized in him, for the shallow humans who scoffed at the Venusians because they had never conquered space and had shamelessly borrowed and stolen the achievements of Earth science in that field. But the scoffers did not realize that Venus had a science of its own. Their science was not so much quantitatively as qualitatively different from Earth's, and its most basic tenets seemed sheer nonsense to an Earthly mind. The Over Race had liberated atomic energy, for example, before the coming of the

Earthmen; but no human scientist had ever fathomed the workings of a Venusian atomic engine. They seemed to regard the subatomic particles as possessed in some fashion of will and purpose, and they coaxed atoms apart with gentle persuasion instead of smashing projectiles.

That much Degnan knew—and he was very far from laughing at the Venusian ultimatum.

He realized with a chill start how close his thinking was coming to the propaganda line he had heard yesterday evening, about the decadence and stupidity of mankind. Had he too soaked up some of that mental virus? And what touchstone would serve to distinguish the ideas native to your mind from those deftly inset by a monstrous psychologist?

WHEN HE got back to his room, the green light on the phone recorder was aglow. From headquarters, a summons to come in for further examination, he thought with an odd stirring of rebellion, and flipped on the speaker.

A woman's voice, hauntingly known to him. "Colonel Degnan—this is Margaret Lusk, who was with you on the *Sheneb*.

"I have to warn you. Something is about to happen—will begin happening very soon, that will be tremendously important to you and through you to—everybody. You must be ready."

The voice changed, became somehow more emotional, more human, and still more familiar. "If you'll meet me this evening at seven, in front of the City Museum—maybe I can tell you something more. I can't promise, because I don't know how I know what I said before…but please come. You've got to come…"

That was all. The recorder hummed unnoticed for a time; finally Degnan spun it back and ran the message off again.

Whatever the quirk in his head was—delusion, premonition—he wasn't alone with it. He had company, and the knowledge was a straw to cling to.

Warmly, though he thought impersonally, he remembered the dark haired girl called Margaret Lusk—ridiculous that he hadn't learned her name before, after all they'd been through together. He felt a queer bond between himself and her, born of a few long, long minutes aboard the *Sheneb*; and he found himself, half-consciously, comparing his memory of her face, ravaged by suffering and terror, with his last glimpse of Athalie—blonde beauty marred by passion, her furious blindness to everything but her own desires. The comparison was in Margaret Lusk's favor.

Above all, though—she might hold the answer, or a part-answer, to the question that was becoming his nightmare.

BEFORE seven o'clock he was marching restlessly up and down in the park grounds before the Museum. In the warm gathering dusk, there were other strollers otherwise preoccupied. Couples arm in arm, walking or sitting on the benches and talking and laughing softly while darkness came over the city.

In the west, above the trees, a bright star shone before the rest—Venus as the evening star. The people in the park saw it, but their gayety was not dampened by it.

As the night came nearer, Venus grew brighter still and the other stars came out, and high up among them brief sparks of light streaked swiftly like the burning pebbles of a meteor shower, and died redly or flared out of existence in soundlessly brilliant explosions. They came as often as one to the minute, in every part of the sky, and Degnan knew what they were—bombardment, rockets from Venus approaching Earth at five hundred or a thousand miles a second, caught and wiped out by the interceptor barrage.

Ahead of him a girl squealed with a tingling thrill of fright and snuggled against the soldier with her, as they saw one flash out brighter than the rest.

"That was a near one," said the soldier gruffly. "Must not have stopped it more than two, three hundred miles up. But," he swelled his chest a little, "we're safe. Not a one's got through, and not a one's going to."

The girl murmured something admiring.

Margaret Lusk was late showing up. Degnan was beginning to wonder if she'd stood him up, or if there had been some mistake in time or place. And then he glimpsed her at the other end of the tree-lined walk he had been pacing. He turned and hurried toward her.

As he came near he saw that it was really her, trim and tidy as he had not seen her before, her dark hair braided neatly about her head. She saw him too, smiled quickly and started to call to him...

A huge and blazing star glided clear across the sky, drenching the Museum's grounds and the whole city in an unholy bath of reddish light. Far to the eastward it touched the Earth, and a second later a mountain of searingly radiant vapor began rising there, boiling higher and higher and turning night to day even as the fire-trail faded.

By that glare, Degnan saw the girl's pale face and wide eyes looking like holes burned in a blanket. He said idiotically, "We're all right. The city wasn't hit."

"It's happened!" she gasped, and he couldn't tell whether her tone was, terror or ecstasy. She stood stiffly beside him but apart, gazing at the rising pillar of fire.

Degnan's ability to think came back; he snapped, "Better get down. Flat on the ground. The shock-wave'll be here before long."

But it was minutes before the ground heaved and shuddered with earthquake. On the heels of the earth-wave came the air-wave, a hurricane in violence, and in its midst the lights in the Museum facade, which had so far burned steadily, went out as something happened to Los Angeles' central power plant. Screams rose then from among the people scattered in the park.

THOUGH Degnan didn't know it then, he had seen the arrival of the first of the hyperspace projectiles, which landed fifty miles east of Los Angeles. The manner of its coming was this:

The great robot brain in Denver, which coordinated the defense barrage over all North America and parts of the Pacific and Atlantic oceans, registered, routine-wise, the approach of a Venusian missile aimed at the West Coast. Nothing unusual; a torpedo of normal size, traveling at the somewhat low velocity of five hundred miles per second. In routine fashion, also, the calculator transmitted the information to its human watchers at the same time that it made the necessary computations and sent out the necessary orders to subsidiary units of the interception network. No special alarm was sounded, since it was a simple piece of work to encompass the projectile's destruction.

To do that, the robot brain in essence set up within its own structure the rocket's flight in space and physically possible evasive maneuvers, correlated with the positions of the mines strewn lavishly in orbits about the Earth. It sent out the signals to set those mines in motion that would carry them across all possible paths of the missile, with their blast guns, their charges of atomic explosive and their seeking, thinking controls.

Within the brain the paths converged, met, and the rocket was destroyed.

But in the reality of space, ten thousand miles out—a detector in the Venusian projectile tripped a switch at the first contact with Earth radar, and threw it into hyperspace drive. And it never reached any of the predicted positions, never encountered the searching beams or the shattering explosions.

The robot brain knew that within a fraction of a second. It rang the alarm, this time, and simultaneously sent the inner belt of mines into action.

By now men were incredulously watching the instruments that registered the hyperspace projectile's flight—or tried to register it; the wild shifting of the needles, the crazy fluctuation of the graphs could not be translated into any meaningful space-time coordinates.

While they stared, helpless, the embattled calculator used its last resort; hundreds of interception rockets, tiny, viciously potent proximity-fused things, left their launching sites and climbed at a hundred thousand gravities' acceleration to meet the enemy.

It evaded them, too, still flying its impossible course, and fell not far from San Bernardino, which together with neighboring Riverside and other towns and villages around, vanished that instant from the face of the Earth. Like most such weapons, the hyperspace projectile bore no explosive warhead; but it struck at five hundred miles a second. It blasted a crater a mile across, and the shock waves from it did much damage in San Diego.

By that time the second one, which landed on Calcutta and killed two million people, was coming in toward the Asiatic sector.

DARKNESS, pallidly relieved by the rising moon, lay with strange silence on the great city. Somewhere, far off, sirens sobbed of disaster.

The girl stood facing Ralph Degnan, her back against a tree-trunk in a vaguely defensive pose. He could not read her face, a white blur in the shadow.

He commanded again, "Think! What more do you know?"

"I don't know," said Margaret Lusk. "I had to send you that message, that's all. Something told me to call you—but not about meeting you here. That was my idea."

"I can guess what 'something' was," growled Degnan. He wanted to question her ruthlessly and to the point, but he was finding it hard to concentrate. Something was churning in his mind struggling toward the light like a formless monster heaving itself to the surface of a swamp. Since the projectile's fall he had felt that—the sense of being about to remember something once known but forgotten.

His outward senses seemed to strain sympathetically toward hyper-acuteness. He thought he heard rustlings round about, a stealthy scuffing of feet in the park shrubbery...

An idea struck him with shocking force. He demanded, "Say! How'd you know where to call me? I only found that room late last night!"

She made no reply, but he heard the quick, suspicious intake of breath.

"Answer me!"

Then the slight sounds he had heard and half-dismissed materialized into a rush of pounding feet from every side at once. Instinctively he ducked and spun around. Someone tackled him round the waist and hung on, and other hands were laid on him. His fists lashed out at indistinct figures, and smote air as often as flesh and bone; he lunged furiously, and had a moment's hope of breaking free before something blunt and hard descended stunningly on his head.

The blow made the joints of his skull creak like rusty hinges, and for a while time stood still. When he began to struggle out of the fog, there was a while when he only wanted to crawl back under it and leave his headache outside.

He grew aware that he was sitting propped up, and the feel of the cushioned seat and its slight movements told him he was in a car. Someone was on each side of him. He thought: I'm getting lots of free rides. Then he realized that this was a ride in the worst sense of the word.

CHAPTER SIX

A BRASSY voice was speaking—Degnan couldn't see, because something like a sack was pulled smotheringly over his face, but he formed an instant dislike for the speaker— "I say get rid of him. Hell! If I'd hit him a little harder, there wouldn't be any argument."

"Nah," said a whining voice that he remembered sharply, from yesterday evening, "you couldn't hit that hard, Clark. His head's so thick, even *they* couldn't pound anything into it."

"Maybe I'll show you if I could," said Clark viciously. "Now, what's wrong with stopping right here and kicking him off a pier? We got enough troubles without him…"

"Will you listen to me?" broke in a voice that chilled Degnan to the bone, for it was the voice of Margaret Lusk. "I tell you, he knows something. He has a command. Or why would I have been told to send him a message?"

Degnan thought dully—slaves of Venus, all of them. I was going to lead them on and find out what they knew about this hypnotic business—so I walked straight into a baited trap. And now I'm supposed to know something they don't!

What, exactly, was he supposed to know…? Oh, yes. Sure. That's right.

He remembered, but not the where and how of his coming to know what he did. It fitted somewhere in that twelve-day blank that he still couldn't fill in consecutively... It was like in the stories where a crack on the head cures the hero's amnesia; but he knew it wasn't that simple.

Clear to him were principles and details of the construction and operation of the Venusians' new weapon, the hyperspace projectile, and of the hyperspace drive in general—a startingly simple modification, simple at least to Venusian minds, of the Earth-invented gravities. It was as plain as if someone had just been explaining it all to him, even the gravitic principles he'd been hazy on before.

The revelation shocked him so that he moved convulsively, and discovered that his wrists were lashed together.

"He's coming to life," announced still another voice beside him.

The girl went on unheeding: "It's obvious *they* have a purpose in this, and we'd be crazy if we disregarded it. They cast him adrift with me in the *Sheneb's* life rocket, close to Earth—and I think he was the one they wanted to be sure got here, and I was just ballast. We've got to wait and see."

"Okay, okay," grumbled the man called Clark. "But I think we're cutting our throats."

Degnan hadn't stirred again; he was slumped between his captors, prey momentarily to a paralyzing horror.

He could imagine what was happening now all over Earth—wherever the Venusians chose to aim their new unstoppable projectiles. Irresistible, yet real and deadly, because the concept of hyperspace as an *otherwhere*, wholly out of touch with here and now, was false; rather, it was an *otherhow*. The great calculators of the Earth's defense centers, and the lesser brains of the barrage, could compute trajectories and probabilities in normal space-time, but the course of a hyperspace missile was utterly unpredictable by normal mathematics. Interception of one of them would be pure lucky accident.

THE CAR stopped. Still blinded, he was pushed roughly out. Even with a hard muzzle thrusting into his back, he had to draw tight rein on the impulse to break away and make a dash for freedom.

He tripped over low steps, heard a door open and smelled close indoor air. The gun prodded him forward a short distance, then Clark's voice behind him ordered, "Turn left."

Degnan sensed that the room was a small one even before someone jerked off the blinder. He found himself facing a beefy red-faced man who stood negligently pointing a heavy gun. Degnan's eyes widened slightly; the gun was a flame pistol, actually a compact, pocket-sized atomic blast, strictly forbidden to civilians.

The room was sparsely furnished with a couple of chairs, a table, and a studio couch; dust of neglect on everything. The single window was shuttered, the ceiling light on, which must mean the power had come back.

Behind Clark's thick figure, Degnan saw the slight one of Margaret Lusk, flanked by his insinuating acquaintance of yesterday and another man, a hollow-eyed, unshaven specimen. The girl's dark gaze rested on Degnan with speculation and, he thought, a touch of compassion.

Clark waggled the flame pistol.

"Okay, fellow. She says you've got a command. What is it?"

Degnan was stonily silent. The truth wouldn't do him any good, and he didn't know enough to risk making up a story. If he could learn a little more about what went on—

Clark scowled. "If we're going to find out anything from this dummy, maybe I'd better persuade him to talk."

"You don't really think that would work?" said the girl coldly.

"Never know what a guy'll take until you try him."

"You make me sick," she said, and Degnan had to marvel despite himself at her air of cool superiority. "I don't know why you had to go after him in the first place. Whatever command he carries with him will be set to function in its own time and way, though he may not know what it is himself—and we may be interfering with the Over Race's plans."

Clark's red face grew shades paler; he backed away from the prisoner, the flame gun jittering in his grip in a way that set Degnan's teeth on edge.

"But we can't let him go," mumbled the big man. "Can we?"

The girl shrugged. "No. But we can keep him here, and try to find out—in an intelligent way—what he's supposed to do."

"How?"

She bit her lip, frowning faintly.

Her gaze traveled searchingly over Degnan's set face, as if trying to read his thoughts. If she could have done so, she wouldn't have found them pleasant; he was nursing the bittersweet thought of getting his hands on her throat. At the moment, it seemed to him that he hated the girl more than the others, as if her betrayal of humanity had wounded him personally and deeply...

She said with decision, "We'll have to try hypnosis."

The other slaves of Venus stared. Clark grunted suspiciously, "Maybe *you* know how to do that?"

MARGARET LUSK nodded confidently. "It's the only way to find out what's in a person's subconscious mind—and that is where the Over Race plant their commands." She picked up a handbag from the table and rummaged in it, came out with something that flashed—a small mirror; she explained, "It's not hard.   You fix their attention with something bright, and... Well, just keep quiet and I'll show you."

She moved to the studio couch and spent a minute or so carefully adjusting its cushions, then beckoned Degnan to sit down.   He obeyed silently, watching her with gathering puzzlement. "That's it. Now lean back. Way back. Relax."

There was an odd tense urgency in her low voice— scarcely the soothing note the hypnotist uses. And the whole show was unutterably phony.   Degnan was no expert on hypnotic technique, but he was familiar enough with it to realize that Margaret knew a good deal less than he... Deliberately he kept his expression impassive, leaned back obediently against the cushions, hands still bound behind him.

She was waving the hand-mirror slowly to and fro in front of his eyes, murmuring, "Relax. Sleep. Go to sleep..." She couldn't really imagine that hocus-pocus would work.   It might conceivably have had an effect on a very cooperative subject; but anybody knew that to put an unwilling victim under you needed drugs or other drastic aids.   Then he noticed from the corner of his eye that the spot of light reflected from the little mirror was dancing erratically on the wall; the hand that held it was trembling.

The others were taken in, though.   They watched open-mouthed, with something of superstitious awe—except Clark, maybe; the big man's eyes were narrowed as they rested on the girl.   But even he had dropped the heavy flame gun into his jacket pocket.

Margaret's dark eyes held Degnan's, and their bright intense gaze mirrored—pleading?   "Go to sleep. You're sinking—down, down—deep into the cushions—"

Degnan's bound hands writhed behind him, while with all his control he strove to remain outwardly immobile. He managed to keep from moving, even when a sharp pain stabbed one of those searching hands. He fumbled further, got hold of the penknife that had been hidden just under the edge of the cushion at his back. It was a little thing, but razor-keen. With Infinite care he began working it between his wrists and the thin, tough cord that held them.

Clark scowled darkly and came forward, hulking and purposeful; he grasped Margaret's arm, and Degnan saw her wince. "You're getting nowhere fast," he growled. "I've seen hypnotism acts, and that's not the way—"

She whirled on him in a fury that must have been real. "Now you've done it. I'll have to start over—"

"I don't know." Clark didn't let loose of the girl. "I'm beginning to wonder just what the hell you're up to."

THERE WOULDN'T be a better chance. Degnan came to his feet in a rush whose impetus was behind the long straight punch he aimed at a point below the big man's ear.

Clark had time to start turning his head, and caught it glancingly on the side of the jaw, but it sent him reeling against the wall. And Degnan, without ever stopping moving, had scooped up a chair and clubbed it down on the fellow who had tried to convert him the day before.

The hollow-eyed one was backing to the far end of the room and tugging out a pistol. Degnan sent the chair rocketing at him with the speed and unavoidability of an artillery shell, and swung around to face Clark, who had come dizzily erect and was clawing at his coat pocket. Degnan tackled him and they crashed to the floor together; Degnan applied the jujitsu methods that were part of his NAMI training, and an instant later the flame gun was in his hand.

As he scrambled clear of the groaning Clark, he heard Margaret's scream blend with a crash of glass. The hollow-eyed man was backed against the further wall with an automatic in his hand, and he had just dodged a thrown table lamp. Without hesitation and almost without aiming, Degnan pulled the trigger.

The concussion was almost stunning in the little room. The air filled chokingly with smoke, and through it flames climbed with a crackling roar, blanketing one end of the room and already blocking the doorway. Degnan snatched up the other chair, found Margaret with his eyes. He shouted, "The window!" and drove the chair—luckily it was a metal-framed one—through glass and shutters. Instantly the fire whipped toward the vent created. Degnan caught Margaret's hand; he shouldered his way through the window, breaking out the remains of the pane, and drew the girl after him.

The night air was cool and sweet. Behind, the house was burning like a torch; some not too scrupulous builder must have used in flammable plastics in it. "Make sure your clothes haven't caught," said Degnan breathlessly, "and come on!" He gestured toward the back, where a weed-grown garden seemed to lead to an alley.

"Wait!" cried Margaret. "Maxon's car's out front."

"That's ri—no; we haven't got the key."

He saw her smile in the glare of the fire. "I have it. I took it off him while you were fighting the others."

"Well, I'll be damned..."

THEY raced round to the front of the burning house. As yet, the noise and blaze didn't seem to have attracted anyone; the nearest dwellings were lightless—perhaps many people had fled the city or taken to their cellars in fear of the hyperspace bombardment, and the police and perhaps the fire department too would be having their hands full tonight.

As he set the car in motion, Degnan said quietly, "Thanks, Margaret. I hope you'll live to know how much this means."

She didn't look at him or answer. Degnan drove slowly for a little while, to avoid being reported fleeing from the scene of the fire; he touched the button that slid back the top of the car, and glanced at the night sky. Overhead, the stars were lost in a murky darkness in which intermittent lightning flickered, weirdly soundless, and once or twice there were long streaks of fire and far thunder. With prescient certainty, Degnan knew that Earth could not long endure the punishment Venus was giving her now... His face grew hard with determination.

He turned onto one of the arterial highways, heading toward the center of the city, and increased speed as much as he dared, until the old car's drive unit whined protest into the whistle of wind.

Margaret said abruptly, "I want you to know—I didn't lead them to you on purpose. They knew where you were, anyway—it was Clark that gave me your address."

Degnan's mouth tightened; he didn't take his eyes off the road. "I still don't get the whole picture. What about these 'commands' of *yours?*"

This time her gaze was steady and fearless upon him. "It was horrible. I just didn't seem to care. Everything was ugly and useless, and I hated everybody and myself most of all... It wasn't hearing voices or anything like that. I just knew what I had to do, and all the time I knew too that something a long way off was pulling the strings and making me do it... Then, when they slugged you, there in the park, something seemed to go 'pop', and I knew *it* had lost control."

"For keeps?"

She held her head high, beautiful in a defiance aimed not at Degnan but at the monstrous thing in her memory. "Sometimes I can feel it trying to creep back like a snake, crawling, trying to wrap itself around me…" She shivered. "But I can brush it away. I'm myself now, and I'm going on being myself."

Degnan was silent, wondering: posthypnotic suggestions, then? Her telepathic sensitivity must be way up there, over a hundred on the Bjornsson scale… His own sensitivity was low, he knew, and he hadn't felt anything like that. In his case there were only memory gaps and memories that weren't real. For the first time it occurred to him that his knowledge of the hyperspace principle might be one of those—but he couldn't believe that; the knowledge was too complete, too logically coherent.

"How'd you come to get mixed up with that gang?"

"I wandered away from the spaceport—I didn't know where I was going. Somebody was following me, I think—"

Degnan nodded, as if to say "naturally."

"Then I met Clark," she continued, "and he showed me how to lose them, and took me to that house where the others were. They told me I'd left my soul on Venus, and it was true, then. Later on they seemed to be afraid of me, because I knew things they didn't…" She paused, passing a hand across her eyes.

INWARDLY, Degnan cursed the Over Race's science. But outwardly he smiled and said, "You're out from under them now. They can make it stick with minds that are off balance already, but they guessed wrong about us."

She gave him a queer, scared look. "I'm free now. But I'm not so sure about you."

"Eh?"

"I told those men I thought you had a command from Venus. I'm still not sure it isn't true."

"If so," said Degnan harshly, "something's gone wrong with their chain of command. They're due for a shock! But if you thought that, why'd you help me get away?"

Margaret's face was in shadow as they passed between lightless rows of houses. "I'm not sure," she said candidly. "I like you, Degnan, and I wanted to help you—but I have a funny impersonal sort of feeling about you, too. As if—you were the most important man in the world."

Degnan smiled tautly. "There your feelings are on the right track. I am."

"What do you mean?"

"That thing that landed east of here tonight—and others like it must be hitting Earth every few minutes. I know what they are and how to stop them, and I've got to make what I know count in time. That's why we're on the way to NAMI headquarters now."

"Oh," was all she said.

He once more admired her control. There on the *Sheneb* he had thought her hysterical; actually she had been sapped by the mental poison the Venusians had administered. Now she was whole again and strong.

"I'm not taking you there," he assured her. "Stop off anywhere you like."

She didn't brighten. "I've nowhere to go; my brother was my only relative," she said tonelessly, and he wondered if she knew the prison ship had been destroyed. "And if any of those men got out of the fire back there—they and the others like them will be after me."

Degnan hesitated momentarily. "Now's not a good time to turn yourself in. Everybody'll be scared half-witted by what's happening and you might get some rough handling. I'm not looking forward to an easy time myself." He came to a quick, illogical decision, assuring himself that what he, and the whole world, owed this girl outweighed the minutes that would be lost. "I've got a room rented for a week in advance and a feeling I won't be using it. There's automatic service; if you don't go out, nobody's likely to even know you're there for a few days, anyway. And when this is over, I'll see you again."

He knew where he was now, and picked a turnoff from the highway without hesitation. In front of the hotel, he pressed the key and some folded bills into her hand, then gave her the flame gun he had taken from Clark, and advised curtly: "If the police find you—better give yourself up and hope for the best. But if your ex-playmates come around—give them fair warning, then push off the safety, like this, and let fly. It'll blow the side out of the apartment but don't let that stop you. You ought to be all right if nothing hits Los Angeles—which it won't, if I get through in time."

On impulse he bent to kiss her goodbye. The kiss lasted longer than it was meant to, with the race for the world's life still ahead.

CHAPTER SEVEN

GENERAL Fleming was restlessly on his feet, pacing aimlessly back and forth as if his roomy office had become a prison cell. The shriveled mask of his face no longer hid the very real fear and uncertainty behind it.

A red-eyed and unkempt Ralph Degnan sprawled in the General's chair and wished the General would stop talking so he could catch a moment's sleep before the flier was ready. It had been a grinding session in the small hours with the handful of mathematicians and engineers he had finally persuaded them to call in—those men, who had been working without sleep on the problem of the hyperspace projectiles, had been at first wearily impatient, not believing, then at the last they had been wide-awake, firing questions at him faster than he could give the answers that were already clear in his mind.

Fleming said abruptly, "I've had our defense potential concentrated over Los Angeles as long as you're still here. Once you get to Combined Fleet Headquarters, you'll be out of danger—about the only place on Earth they still can't touch. It's been more than six hours now since they sent over any of those damn things, but no telling when it will start again. God, how I'd like to think they'd used up their supply... Maybe those devils are just getting something new ready. We stopped over half of them during the last hour's bombardment, and deflected most of the rest. But we've fired three months' ammunition in four and a half hours. Our production can't begin to fill the gap. You've got to be right!"

Degnan said nothing. General Fleming worried on: "I can't understand why human operators, working by guess, can stop them oftener than the machines."

"The calculators are logical," said Degnan. "And so is the path of a body in hyperspace. But it's a different logic. That's all 'hyperspace' means—a different set of rules from those that apply to normal space and energy and matter, the rules man's been learning and building machines by for thousands of years. Our robot brains work according to those rules, so they can't determine the trajectory of a hyperspace projectile."

The General shook his head bewilderedly.

"Our physics has been devoted to determining the characteristics of space, which to the Venusian psychophysicists means the behavior habits of energy and matter," explained Degnan wearily. "They found that other behavior patterns are possible. The difference is a question of energy levels. When a projectile changes to hyperspace drive, it loses about one kilogram of mass, which means enough energy to shake a planet. That's related to the variation in limiting velocities—incidentally, we can use this principle to travel faster than light, or the Venusians can, if—" He stopped.

The General frowned, grasped at a reality he could understand. "Colonel Degnan—I think I can admit now that you were right about the reason for delay in our offensive."

Degnan smiled faintly. "The big powers were afraid their handsome warships would get dented?"

"Not anymore, by heaven! Last word from CFHQ says the delegates took just one quarter of an hour to reach a unanimous decision after the second projectile landed. All fleets made fully available. The offensive is being mounted now—"

A phone on the General's desk buzzed. He snatched it up, listening for a moment without answering, and turned on Degnan with the receiver in his hand. "On your way! Your clearance has come through and the flier will be ready by the time you're on the field..."

DEGNAN'S memory preserved in photographic, nightmarish detail one glimpse of Los Angeles Spaceport as he skirted the field with his guards.

Far out beyond the girdling fence, four great black warships loomed ready for takeoff and rendezvous with the gathering fleets. Above them the sky was turbulent, murkily luminous; Earth was slowly veiling her face in the smoke and dust of her own destruction, the reek of shattered cities and ruined countrysides.

Between the fence and the field itself, under a glare of floodlights, seethed a mass of people, men and women almost equally mixed. They were the same people Degnan had seen in the streets and parks of the city, walking by twos and laughing unafraid in their security. Now, a confused crying rose over them, a voice of tears and lamentation.

Women clung to their men, summoned this hour to duty, and wept and would not let them go to space and the deadly ships and the horror of airless or flaming death millions of miles from anything. And the men—were leaving wives and sweethearts on a world grown perhaps less safe than the gundecks of a warship.

Along the fence ranged stiffly a line of robot marines, armored bodies gleaming coldly under the lights, waiting mindlessly for orders from the mustached officer who stood beside them and watched the scene with an air of bleak dissatisfaction.

As Degnan and the two Intelligence agents with him hurried past, the officer turned his back on the crowd. Drops of sweat glistened on his expressionless face as he snapped an order to the motionless machines. The line of seven-foot robots pivoted with inhuman precision and moved on the swarm of humans, against and among them. Their steel arms flashed and thrust, separating those who must go from those who stayed behind, with the efficiency of a mechanical sorter...

One of the men with Degnan muttered something under his breath. The other said, "They ought to stop that. They shouldn't let those women come this far: they go crazy when they see the ships. It's bad for morale."

"Oh, dry up!" said the other.

Degnan said nothing. His dark face was rock-hard as he led them both across the field toward the flier that waited, dwarfed by the vastness of the interplanetary cruisers.

One of his escorts—the one who had said, "Oh, dry up!"—went aboard with him, the other returned to report that they'd got him safely that far.

GLANCING out through the heavy glass of a window, Degnan became aware that, above the artificial lights of the field, the sky was beginning to flush with rose and delicate violet. Not a minute later, when the flier was many miles above the Earth and racing westward, that had become a red and murky dawn, the dust of battle diffusing sunlight and turning itself into the likeness of smoke from hell's furnaces.

Westward, out over the Pacific they flew. Degnan turned to the man beside him, "Where we headed? Asia?"

The agent shrugged; Degnan guessed that he honestly didn't know. Combined Fleet Headquarters was the secret of secrets—Earth's hidden nerve center, housing the top military staffs and the top scientists who could—perhaps— still make use of Degnan's special knowledge in time.

Degnan had firmly intended to sleep through the flight, but a gnawing unrest kept him wide awake now. Deliberately he lit a cigarette; by the time it was smoked down the flier might be over China. He found himself alternately glancing at his watch and staring with smarting eyes out the window, into the flaming cauldron of clouds that brightened as the ship rose higher, then began fading again as its flight outran the sunrise. His imagination did strange things with it, turned it into something terrible, a burning wind and fire that swept over the face of the Earth and left lifeless desert behind. The Over Race's final weapon, with which their radio had threatened Earth again last night...

Probably a bluff, he told himself angrily. And why should it occur to him now? He could do nothing that he was not doing already—going at a dozen miles a second to save Earth from the hyperspace bombardment.

But why the deadly pressure behind his racing thoughts, the cold knot of fear in his stomach, his sense that the sands were running out?

A change of pitch in the high screaming of thin air outside told him the ship was going down, probably slowing as well toward a landing. It rocked and swerved a little, battered by the changing pressures of a too-swift descent, and Degnan glimpsed a vast sweep of ocean, glittering in faint moonlight, unbroken by any land. All at once he remembered that these gravitic fliers could travel under water as well, and he knew where Combined Fleet Headquarters was—under the bottom of the Pacific, below one of the great deeps. The only place on Earth, sheltered under all that cushioning water, that no interplanetary bombardment could reach. There might have been a political motive for the choice of location, too; the oceans had belonged to no nation since the first feeble international laws were set up.

A MINUTE or two left. The roar of riven air grew louder, more ominous—like the whistle of a shell prolonged intolerably, for a lifetime before the explosion thunders, like the scream of a falling bomb—

A bomb was falling, howling and shrieking its tuneless death song before it blew itself into nothingness and took with it the whole Earth, everything, everything that had been good and bad and indifferent in the world of man. Its crescendo noise swelled and beat against the confines of Degnan's skull, drowning the one silent sound that he had to hear.

Something in his brain was struggling, beating on a closed and barricaded door, shouting incoherently into the clamor of the descending bomb. Degnan saw only the sweeping second-hand of his watch. He had to understand, to remember before that hand went round once or twice again and it was too late forever and ever.

Something was coming up out of the abyss of darkness and drugged forgetfulness. The gleam of his watch-face transformed itself into the pitiless shining eyes of a great Venusian, eyes cold and burning with knowledge and passionless will.

It was a scientist and a ruler—one of the masters of the Over Race, who would some day be masters of the Universe. As man had foolishly dreamed...

"Forget," it seemed to drone in the travesty of human speech that was the best their voice-converters could make of Venusian speech-sounds. "Forget one minute longer, and the experiment will succeed. Go on. You cannot fail. We cannot fail."

It lied. With a savage effort of will, he wiped the vision out of existence. And as it vanished, the floodgates of memory were opened, and he knew—what Venus had planned, what he had been about to do.

As Degnan's sight cleared, he found himself on his feet, swaying like a drunken man. Before him danced a face, that of his escort, whom he must have pushed aside as he stood up—a shocked stare, dawning suspicion: "What's the matter with you?"

Degnan faltered only a moment. With merciless clarity he realized the impossibility of explaining to this man, or any other, in the time that was left; with regret, but with brutal purposefulness, he hit the agent on the point of the jaw and saw the man fall down limply.

The pilot had still less warning. Degnan struck one skillful, chopping blow and snatched at the control bar; through the nose window he saw the steely glint of waves sliding swiftly nearer, and yanked. He felt nothing, of course, through the full-gravity thrust drive. But now there was only the night sky in the window, and he knew the flier was climbing almost vertically. Only then did he heave the half-stunned pilot out of his seat and into the aisle of the passenger compartment.

HE SANK into the seat, breathing hard, momentarily incapable of further thought or action. Through timeless intervals, the sky's turbid darkness gave place to a hard, crystal-clear blackness, and in it the stars came out and shone with unwinking brilliance. On the control panel an alarm buzzed stridently and a red light winked on and off. That meant the flier was approaching the danger limit for unshielded atmospheric craft, radiation in the space around it becoming dangerous to life. Still, it was a while before Degnan stirred to shift the controls and drop Earthward again.

He leveled out in the stratosphere, recovering from shock and beginning to think furiously. There was no hiding here, high up in air; within minutes, at most, an alarm would be out and radar tracers searching for the flier. Overpowering the other, seizing the ship had been an almost instinctive reaction of self-preservation; it made no real difference in his position. He was outlawed anyway, exiled from Earth now and forever by the strangest and most terrible fate a man had ever suffered.

Behind him someone groaned, beginning to come to. Almost without looking around. Degnan slammed and locked the door of the pilot's compartment. Clinging desperately to sanity, he tried to form a plan.

He knew now the nature of the Venusians' final weapon. He was that weapon.

Every atom of his body, every particle of flesh and blood and bone was a grain of explosive waiting for the flash of a detonator.

Earthmen had known, without thoroughly understanding, that the Over Race's science could convert any inorganic substance into fissionable material without changing its overt physical or chemical properties; for that reason, import of articles from Venus had been rigorously supervised. They had not known, the enemy had carefully kept them from finding out that the same thing could be done with living matter. The Venusian liberation of nuclear energy was inferior, in ergs returned for ergs invested, to Earth's use of the power metals—but it had the one decisive advantage in war, that a Venusian atomic bomb could take any form, even that of a living, breathing man. *The one form in which it would surely pass Earth's defenses and find its way—*

Degnan remembered what the detonating impulse was to have been. A simple and thoroughly Venusian device. His arrival—his own realization that he had arrived—at CFHQ would have been the trigger.

Mass times the velocity of light squared—he tried briefly to calculate the force of explosion, and recoiled from the figures that suggested themselves. At the very least, Earth's vital center would have vanished into dust together with cubic miles of the planet's surface.

HE COULDN'T go back. If he were taken to CFHQ, even his conscious knowledge of what was to come would not check the automatic reaction. Even his lifeless body must not return to Earth. It was that thought, largely, that had kept him from heading the flier on into space and the burning bath of radiation; the defense patrol would intercept it and bring him back, alive or dead. He couldn't imagine that there was any alternative way of setting off the explosion, any control that could reach across space from Venus—but the danger was too great for any chance to be taken.

Also, he was not the kind of man to display suicidal courage until every other kind of courage had failed.

The Venusians had known him well, he realized sickly, when they had chosen him. They had planned every step ahead, foreseen everything, when they had arranged his "escape" from the *Sheneb,* his return to Earth with the knowledge they had deliberately planted in his mind, knowledge important enough to make sure he would be sent to CFHQ—latent, triggered into consciousness by the fall of the first hyperspace projectile. Perhaps they had even made sure to see that he would be in the open to see that by inspiring Margaret Lusk to make a date with him in the park; at all events, her call had been a psychological primer, to put him in a receptive mood. His capture by the Venusians' slaves, to be sure, had been a cross-up in their scheme—it showed, what might be important, that they didn't have direct mental control over the humans they had worked on—but it had made little difference. They had known he would get through; they had chosen their instrument with perfect understanding of human psychology... But, no—their plan had failed at the last moment, when the mental blocks they had used on Degnan had gone down by a miracle he was still too dazed to question. There was still room to hope.

Drenched in cold sweat, Degnan stared at the gleaming dials and knobs before him, the paling sky beyond the nose of the flier. He had headed it mechanically back the way it had come, toward the North American coast. And now an idea began to glimmer... He would be risking not only his own life (forfeit already!) but many others besides; yet on the other hand... Convulsively he leaned forward and spun the power rheostat as far as it would go.

The line of shore was featureless in the light of a gray dawn, encroaching on the oily darkness of the sea. Degnan braked the flier swiftly and swooped lower, finding partial orientation by the lights that still shone sickly here and there, where Los Angeles sprawled to southward.

At last he located the little bay he knew. Rummaging hastily in a storage compartment, he found the automatic pistol stowed there as per some ancient regulation having to do with mutiny on shipboard; he thrust it into a trousers pocket. He cast his coat aside, and dropped the flier still lower. When it drifted at a bare twenty miles an hour only a few feet above still deep water not far offshore, he flung open the emergency door, took a deep breath and in the same motion pulled back on the control bar and leaped clear.

CHAPTER EIGHT

WHEN HE broke the surface, striking out for the beach, he dashed the water from his eyes and saw the flier already far away, climbing and vanishing into the gray-rose sky. The farther it traveled before it was picked up, the less help it would be to the men who shortly would be combing the planet to find him.

If they could know not only where he was but *what* he was—there would probably be a mass exodus from Los Angeles right now. He reflected grimly that, if the worst were realized, if there were an open switch on Venus that would be closed when the enemy grew tired of waiting, Los Angeles would get it whether he was there or not. He had stayed there two days—and a nail paring of his, a stray hair from his head, would be enough to level city blocks.

He splashed ashore and broke into a jogging run that, weary as he was, he could keep up for the short distance he had to go.

As he ran, the Earth seemed to groan beneath his steps with a premonition of catastrophe.

He couldn't go to the authorities again; with horrible vividness he pictured himself trying to explain to them, being called crazy and shipped back, a prisoner, drugged perhaps, to CFHQ so the scientists there could pick his brains. But he had to have help, and he was going to the only place on Earth where help might be.

The wide white house came into sight as he rounded a bend in the beach road. Built in the rambling California style, among pruned green gardens on a rise of ground, it had a view of the sea from its flat roof—the roof where, on a warm night with a great moon silvering the Pacific, he had gotten engaged to Athalie, once in a world that was far away and unreal. Tonight, if tonight ever came, there would be no moon.

But Athalie was there. He found her—having flung open the unlocked door and plunged inside without ceremony, in a sudden fear lest the house be as deserted as it looked—in the spacious living room; she was huddled in a big chair, against the wall opposite the great windows that looked eastward across the dunes, staring out at the brightening sunrise.

She didn't seem to see him standing in the doorway. He called hoarsely, "Athalie!"

The girl raised her head, saw him, and sprang to her feet in a quick scared motion. She took a recoiling step.

"It's me. Ralph." He came toward her, and she did not retreat again, but her gaze on him was feverish and blank. There were sleepless shadows under her eyes, her bright hair was unkempt, her makeup smudged, some of her fingernails broken and untrimmed. Half-consciously Degnan noted those details and could not understand, until he remembered that she, like all Earth, had gone through the night of terror, the hours of the hyperspace bombardment. He hesitated. "Is your father here?"

She shook her head, said painfully, "He went with the Fleet. He had a reserve commission, and he got them to take him. He went on one of the battleships—I don't remember which one."

DEGNAN was prey to a sinking feeling. He would greatly have preferred, just now, to talk to Charles Norton, who was his friend and whose combination of hardheadedness and imagination he respected... But Athalie

65

would have to do. Certainly the quarrel they'd had counted for less than nothing now.

He said with an uncontrollably pounding heart, "And your father's yacht—did it go out with the Fleet?"

"No. The guns weren't ready, or something. What do you want?" she demanded uncomprehendingly.

"I want that ship," said Degnan, and the way he said it made her take another backward step. Her lips moved and relaxed without framing a question. "It's still on his field? Guarded?"

She nodded and finally got out, "Why?"

He ignored the query. His whole being was centered on the need to get that ship—perhaps the only space-going vessel left on Earth now which had a full-gravitic drive, which might carry him through Earth's defense and out of reach... "Listen. They'll let you in to look at the ship, won't they? And maybe me with you. You've got to help me get to the *Azor's* controls."

She went on staring at him; then a spark of the old strong-willed Athalie flared up. "You must be crazy! Where have you been? What's happened? What can you possibly—"

He took a deep breath, realizing the strange figure he must be—drenched from head to foot, haggard, the awful burden he carried showing in his face. "I want to go to Venus," he said, and regretted it the same moment; now he would have to explain, and he had hoped to get Athalie's help without that.

"Now I know you're crazy. Venus! Nobody can go to Venus. The Venusians are coming here..." She broke; her body shook with sobs, but her eyes were dry and over-bright.

He might have tried to comfort her, but somehow the strength wasn't in him. He stood gazing down at her, and in terse sentences, jealous of the time that was trickling through his fingers—in a toneless voice, as one telling a story already grown old, he related what had happened since yesterday evening; told her why he must go to Venus, or failing that at least leave Earth, if he died in the attempt.

She quieted, and as he finished, shrank back against the wall, pressing her hands against it. His eyes bored into her, seeking; but he could not tell whether she believed or not.

AFTER A silence that was not long, but seemed so, Athalie said, "But even if it's true—it doesn't make any difference. Everything's over anyway. We—Earth is going to surrender."

"The hell you say!"

She nodded abstractedly, as if he had agreed. "It was on the radio a few minutes ago. A message from Venus: if we don't surrender, they'll start the bombardment again at one o'clock. We couldn't stand it—you see that, don't you? They broadcast the message, because the censorship is down— we've all got to make up our minds now. And the Nations' delegates are meeting to decide."

The world seemed to rock around Degnan. He muttered hoarsely, "The Fleets…"

"They can't win. The radio didn't say that, of course—but everybody knows it's hopeless." She straightened suddenly and grasped at his arm with nervous strength, her manner fevered again. "Ralph! The Venusians have promised to let some people go, to live on Mars. They'll let us go if they think we're on their side. Help me think, Ralph—how can we make them understand we're in favor of surrendering?"

For a moment Degnan felt hollow, sick and weak inside; he realized how tired he was… He set his teeth and caught Athalie by both shoulders in a grip that made her cry out sharply. "That's enough of that! Mankind isn't ready to quit yet. And you—you'll do one last thing for your own world before you start bowing and scraping to Venus!"

Athalie had wilted. He felt her trembling, knew it was fear of him and did not relent. Nothing mattered now except his purpose.

There was a half-mad light in the eyes that met his—or perhaps they only reflected his own. She faltered, "Don't, don't—I will."

He let her go, feeling at last a touch of pity for her. Last night had shattered her brittle self-confidence, left her subject to only one motive: fear.

He ordered, "Take me to the *Azor*."

It was Degnan who took the wheel of Athalie's sky-blue speedster and pushed it at savage speed over the road that wound along the shore. But as Charles Norton's one-time private landing field came in sight, he slowed and flung at the girl:

"I'll be an engineer friend of yours, who wants to see— informally—if the ship mightn't be usable after all. I can talk some technical language, and you vouch for me... At least they'll be thrown off guard."

There had been a low fence around the field when he had seen it last; the military had heightened that and topped it with barbed wire. One gate was closed and barricaded; beside the other one, a flimsily-built guardhouse. And beyond the fence—the *Azor*, its once golden hull painted space-black, a spidery temporary scaffolding about it. Work was evidently at a standstill now. They wouldn't have touched the engines, though; and even if the ship weren't sealable he could fly it in a vacuum suit.

HE WAS WELL aware that he had no chance of getting to Venus alive. But he knew the *Azor* of old, knew what its powerful drivers would do; there would be an excellent chance of shooting past the units of Earth's defense patrol that had not been drawn off by the offensive, into deep space, and once out there—set a collision course for Venus and give the engines full power. By the time the fuel was exhausted, the ship would have a velocity of over five thousand miles a second. Even if it were blasted to fragments when it hit the Venusians' barrage, the fragments would still have the momentum of its two thousand tons.

And if that death plunge should carry him close enough to the enemy world— There was a question which, when it first occurred to him, he had hastily crammed back into the darkest recess of his mind; he brought it into the light now. If he were to think, with deliberate conviction: I am at Combined Fleet Headquarters—now!—would that thought set off the reaction, before the brain censor could label it a lie?

He set the brakes in front of the gateway and reached for the door-button, eyes still fixed hungrily on the space ship. Then a scuffing sound jerked his head around—and he saw the car's other door already open, and Athalie outside, running, stumbling across the sand toward the guardhouse, crying shrilly, "Help! Help! There's a crazy man out here!"

For only an instant, Degnan sat stunned. The thought streaked through his head: I should never have looked away. If I'd only kept my eyes on her she'd never have dared— But there was no time for regrets. A uniformed figure had appeared at the door of the guard-shack, and the sun flashed on metal in its hands.

Degnan slammed full power into the drive unit and spun the wheel; the car whipped round with violence that almost blacked him out. There was only one way to go and that was back, a quarter mile of naked shore before the road dipped from sight, and he took that road at a hundred, a hundred and fifty miles an hour, tires screaming on the curves. He thought he heard a shout behind; but he was counting on the fellow not shooting before he found out what was up. For a wild moment, he had thought of crashing the fence; but then the guard would certainly have opened fire.

The rising ground hid him, and he released held breath. But he didn't slacken the deadly pace for half a mile more; then, within sight of the Norton house, he swung the car off the road, careening into the ditch where it would be partly shielded from aerial view by a couple of scrubby pines, and sprang out. His weary muscles responded poorly, but he drove himself into a dogged run—inland, toward the city.

Within minutes the hunt would be up—on the ground, in the sky, many against one, and sometime the lone quarry must stop, rest, while the ring closed in...

Skirting a tree-bordered road, he slowed at last to a walk. The road and the air above seemed deserted, but he kept under cover of the trees. Ahead, the sun climbed higher—a weird sun, a white disk through the high pall of dust that hung over the Earth.

SOMETIME later, he was in an outlying business center; normally its streets would have already been crowded at this hour, but today there were few people, and those hung in knots on the street-corner or crept aimlessly about, glancing up in furtive fear at the pallid sky. Among them, Degnan's bedragglement and his haggard look was not conspicuous; his clothes had finished drying as he ran, and he had halted briefly to brush away the incrusted salt. He breathed more deeply; by losing himself among Los Angeles' millions, he would at least gain a little time.

Much further on, in a little park, he crept beneath a dense thicket of bushes to rest. The leaves sagged tiredly under a film of sooty dust, and as the day wore on it was growing crushingly hot, as before a thunderstorm. At one o'clock—

With continuing effort Degnan held himself just above the edge of sleep, letting his body rest while his mind stayed feverishly awake. Could he ever sleep again? For he might dream— An hour or more by the white sun he lay there— his watch had stopped since his plunge into the sea—and at the end of that time got stiffly to his feet and went on. Aimlessly now, for there was no use trying to put more distance between himself and the point where he had last been seen—the point around which they would have drawn a circle, within which he must be. Perhaps they already knew, by a process of elimination, that he had gone into the city.

He knew now that no one on Earth would believe his story. Athalie... She had not believed—not that it would have made any difference; she was too far-gone in hysteria. She hadn't even been scheming to get him caught, back there; she had only been running away.

Here and there on the streets he saw pairs and groups of new citizen militia, grim-faced, with armbands and rifles, often accompanied by regular police robots. The night just past must have created a problem of order the regular forces couldn't handle; there would be many that, like Athalie, had lost their heads completely, and their panic could take unpleasant forms. Human civilization had been shaken to its roots. And over every effort to hold it upright now lay the shadow—the new Venusian ultimatum.

Somewhere on Earth, out there under the Pacific, no doubt, the United Nations' delegates were meeting under that shadow. And in each of them—the poisonous thought: "They've promised to spare a few. If one should speak out now for surrender—"

Those men would surely reject such a motive with revulsion. But there was another, more insidious thought: "Man's time has come, to go the common way of a million other species, of the dodo and the tyrannosaur—outclassed and replaced. What use to struggle against a higher life form?"

CHAPTER NINE

IN ALL THE millennia of his blundering, bloody history, man had achieved no more than the vision of detached intelligence, emancipated from the blind compelling forces that rose constantly out of his unconscious to mock him with apehood. The unconscious is the larger part of *Homo sapiens'* mind; there had been dreams of a *Homo superior* to come some day... But the Over Race had such intelligence *now*.

Some Earthly psychologists had claimed—and the Venusians had never denied—that the brain of the Over Being was actually inferior, in absolute potential, to the human. But their potential intelligence was one hundred per cent realized and uninhibited by feelings; it wasn't that they lacked emotional drives, but their emotions were on the conscious level, the intellect dominant.

The history of Venus was relatively short, as the Over Race was a recent mutation of their lesser kin whose psychic structure resembled that of men. But that history was one single purposefully rising curve, without the wave rings and cyclic reversions of man's past; on Venus there had been no dark ages, no great divisions and wars. In the absence of those factors, which had made introspection a hissing and a byword among Earthly psychological methods, the science of mind had led technical achievement—but that too had advanced on the rising curve. That the first ships to cross space had been Terrestrial was perhaps only an accident; under their cloud blanket the Venusians had had little idea of astronomy, no direct knowledge of stars and planets.

That was a basic environmental difference. Through all his wanderings and dark ages, man had seen the stars overhead, and dreamed dreams; he had been at last almost ready to reach out for the stars...

That was the last and greatest prize at stake in this last war: the right to fulfill that human dream. Only for the Venusians, if they won, it would be no such fulfillment, but only another episode in the smooth mechanical functioning of their total intelligence.

Yet, for all their superiority, they had made one basic mistake in the field where they were strongest; Degnan, on whom the error had been made, could recognize it now. They had wholly misunderstood the duality of the human mind, supposed that knowledge erased from the conscious would no longer affect the subject's motives or actions. But human psychologists, who had fumbled at the gates of the unconscious for centuries, knew that to it belonged the complex of blind forces which the old theologians had called "conscience", and to which various names had been given since Freud's pioneer hypotheses; by any name it was the same, a power greater in the end than merely conscious reason or will. The Over Race could not be expected to see that; their mentality was by definition conscienceless...

THE SIGHT of a squad of armed militiamen jarred Degnan out of a sleepwalking bemusement and made him step quickly into the doorway of a cafe, to busy himself holding matches to a waterlogged cigarette. The cafe was open, and he glimpsed a lighted television screen inside; he realized then two of his own most immediate problems—he must eat if he were to have the strength to keep going, and he must know whether a general alarm had gone out for him.

In the latter he was almost incredibly lucky. He had scarcely collected a hasty meal and sat down inconspicuously in a corner—fortunately the cafe was an automat—when the screen blazed with an announcement, at once printed and spoken for extra emphasis:

"The persons whose pictures will be shown immediately following are slaves of Venus and traitors to Earth. They are believed to be somewhere in this city. All citizens are requested to watch for them and assist in their capture dead or alive."

A series of over a dozen pictures, with names, ages, other data, displayed for a minute or two apiece. Among them Degnan recognized the red-faced Clark; and last in the series was Margaret Lusk. Degnan's heart contracted strangely as her image filled the screen; it was a moving picture, breathtakingly real, and it must have been taken some time ago, before she had gone to Venus, for in it she was smiling with a carefree gayety he had never seen in the brief time he had known her, and in the background were glimpses of a summer landscape of Earth...

Then a repetition of the announcement. "The persons whose pictures have just been shown...Dead or alive!"

Degnan bitterly regretted not having advised the girl to go straight to the police. But everything had seemed so simple then. Now—it wasn't likely to make any difference to her, or anybody else, before long, anyway.

The important thing was that they hadn't broadcast his picture. Perhaps that meant they still hadn't come to a decision about what was behind his disappearance; certainly, at least, it meant they wanted him alive.

If they caught him, it wouldn't be alive. It was as good as certain now that his dead body would be harmless, that the only trigger was a perceptive reaction in his living brain. By now the Venusians, as their new ultimatum showed, had written their "final weapon" off the books and were going on to victory without it.

Degnan froze; the telescreen now showed a news announcer, and "the Fleets" had come crashing into his consciousness.

THE ANNOUNCER'S face had an ill-hidden strained, hunted look. "…that military operations which began around Venus at eight o'clock Pacific Time had practically ceased. Some units of the Combined Fleets, including a number of cruisers and lighter craft, were reported regrouping between Venus and the Sun, with a good chance of returning safely to Earth. The two battleships, *San Ch'ieh* and *Yucatan*, previously thought to have escaped the Venusian barrage, are now definitely known to have been lost…"

Mechanically, Degnan glanced at the clock beside the telescreen. It was eleven o'clock; three hours since the Fleets had contacted the enemy.

And it was evident that the Fleets had been destroyed. At the moment he didn't even care much about learning the details; he only half listened as the announcer went on, in a taut unnatural voice, briefly reviewing the disastrous Battle of Venus. Little enough was known—only that the Over Race had produced some new and frightful wizardry, that Earth ships had exploded and disintegrated in apparently clear space still a quarter of a million miles from the enemy world, attacked by something that neither ordinary equipment nor that hastily rigged up to cope with hyperspace missiles could detect or fend off. With what he alone knew, Degnan could guess at the nature of that attack. A variation on the hyperspace principle, pulsating fields projected by devices too small to register on detectors until it was too late; the ships must have torn themselves apart as portions of their structures ceased to obey the same physical laws as the rest…

Within those three hours the last of the great battleships, Earth's pride and power, were dead. One of those ships, given ten minutes inside the enemy's defenses, could have reduced the part of Venus inhabited by the Over Race to something resembling the surface of the Moon; but they had never had a chance to get that near, had never, after the first contact, had even a chance to win free again.

With a shrinking foreboding, Degnan glanced round him, covertly studying the faces of the other people in the cafe. In them he did not find the shock and unwillingness to believe that he felt himself—but then these people had, no doubt, heard earlier reports and had time to grow familiar with catastrophe. He did see an ominous blankness, a helpless, hopeless fixity in the eyes that watched the screen, that might mean resigned despair—might mean the end. If people like these, a couple of billion of them in all the lands of Earth, were ready to give up, it would be their decision that counted. The delegates' votes would be cast according to what the observers in their various countries reported on the state of mass feeling, on the results of hurried surveys, the resolutions of local political organizations... It was obvious that, as Athalie had said, the censorship had been removed, complete freedom of information restored; that at least was a heroic gesture in what might be man's last hour.

DEGNAN compelled himself to finish eating and drinking, and went into the streets again, under the veiled noonday sun. He had to keep going—the more nearly he was approaching the end of his strength, the more surely he had to keep moving; if he stopped for long, he might sleep, and in sleeping be captured. But as long as he was awake and in command of himself—Degnan's hand tightened on the pistol that reposed in his pocket.

He wasn't much worried about the militia now, and was sure he had nothing to fear from the bulk of the people he passed, or who passed him by—merely wandering aimlessly, like him, or going mechanically about business that no longer mattered. He wondered what they would do, if they knew what walked among them—run screaming for non-existent safety, or merely stand rooted in a numbness beyond fear?

The pale sun had passed the zenith; the air hung dusty, hot and heavy as the air before a storm, unshaken in the abnormal silence that layover the city. But in that silence Degnan heard suddenly an explosion of voices, a murmur that rose and swelled with bursting tension. He saw a cluster of people on the street corner ahead. They pressed round a news-vending machine; sheets fluttered, were snatched and torn as the crowd jostled and grew.

Degnan sensed that the storm had already broken. Careless for the moment of attracting attention, he grasped an arm on the outskirts of the mob: "What's up?"

The man turned with an unseeing stare, then gestured at a paper that was held briefly aloft by someone, its headline vivid:

U.N. REJECTS VENUS DEMAND

Somehow he was a couple of blocks further on, hearing the same story from a public news screen. Ten minutes ago the Nations' delegates had voted unanimously against surrender; perhaps their decision had been made much earlier, but they had delayed, gaining time.

The crowd collected in front of the screen blocked the street, but even now, after the first stirring, they were surprisingly quiet. Most of them wore the same still, set expression that Degnan had seen and tried to analyze before, but now, looking from one to the other, he saw those faces with new eyes. Resigned they were—resigned to suffer and die if it must be, without shouting and fanfares, but not to yield.

And in him rose a feeling long unfamiliar—a sweet and poignant sense of pride in his own kind. If man were about to pass into extinction, he would not go like the dodos that bowed their heads under the clubs, but as the last tyrannosaur or the last saber-toothed tiger must have perished—fighting.

DEGNAN felt clearheaded once more, stronger; it was as if a part of his burden and weariness had been taken from him. The spirit of Earth's peoples, expressed in that unanimous vote—even if their unity should mean no more now than that of the Five Nations of the Iroquois or of Sitting Bull's confederacy had meant against the white man's rifles—was something to remember to the very end.

Someone in the crowd shouted, loud above the rustle of voices, and pointed into the sky; and many, Degnan among them, looked up in time to see a great band of fire that fell through the overcast, seemed for a moment striking at the city, then veered away and vanished into the west.

The voices blended in a long sigh. The torment had begun again, and this time there would be no reprieve… Presently there were other flashes in the clouds: moanings and whistlings far up in air, the hurtling fire-trails of last-ditch interception missiles rising from Earth itself. With what the defenders had learned and the preparations that must have been made in over twelve hours' respite, it should be possible, for a time, to destroy most of the enemy projectiles or at least deflect them away from the great population centers; it might even be days before the world's defensive stores were exhausted. But it would be folly to hope that the Over Race was not ready to carry on the bombardment for as long as they needed to.

Degnan stood motionless, face upturned like the rest; but inside him was a sudden turmoil. It was as if the sight of that first fireball had tripped a spring in his head, even as a similar spectacle had the previous evening—but then the spring had been set by Venus. This time was different; there was no flash of memory lighting up the dark places of his mind, but facts he knew long since were falling into place with swift precision—and one of those facts was that his mind held the mental power to self-detonate himself.

Abruptly he whirled, pushed his way ruthlessly out of the crowd, and began to run.

He pounded through deserted streets and past other skyward-staring groups clustered round the news centers, while above the lightning flickered, up there where the Battle of Earth was being fought. He no longer saw it. Before him danced images from memory, and most constant among them was the vision of Margaret—a queerly superimposed picture, that, of her face as he had seen it last in reality, shadowed by horror past, and as she looked at him from the screen, smiling unafraid in a world that was gone. And in his ears was the echo of words she had spoken last night.

And there was a mathematical certainty. The end of the first hyperspace bombardment had come shortly before midnight—bare minutes after Degnan had arrived at NAMI headquarters. For some six hours, then, the Venusians had held their fire without explanation.

To Degnan the reason was clear. They had discontinued the assault lest it interfere with the functioning of their final weapon. Forced at last to assume that something had gone wrong, they had sent the ultimatum, allowing another quarter-day for its acceptance, during which Degnan might still conceivably accomplish their plan. And now at last they had given him up...

But they could not have known what time he got to the NAMI office. No matter how uncanny their ability to foresee probabilities—and they had shown it amply in the scheme they had built around him—they couldn't have calculated that closely, if for no other reason than that his involvement with their own agents would have upset all timetables.

Unless—

Margaret saying: *"Sometimes I can feel it trying to creep back..."*

If that had been a post-hypnotic effect, it meant nothing. But if it were what she had seemed to think it was, if she had been—possessed—by an alien mind millions of miles away, on Venus—then the Venusians could have known through her. It seemed impossible, but it made the picture complete. Degnan had judged her telepathically sensitive; and now he could guess, for the first time, why she had been returned to Earth with him.

And she had helped him escape—why? Degnan winced. But it didn't matter. What mattered now was to find her, use her in one last attempt...

CHAPTER TEN

AS DEGNAN ran, there settled on his shoulders a new burden of responsibility, and that which he had had to bear before seemed light. For he was about to take the fate of worlds deliberately into his own hands.

Pounding heart and straining lungs told him he couldn't keep up this pace much longer—and there must be miles to go. He was still only roughly oriented in the unfamiliar section of the city to which his wanderings had led him. Grudgingly, he slowed to a rapid walk. Public transportation seemed to have vanished, and there were very few vehicles of any kind moving. Degnan glanced wistfully at the occasional parked cars, but to appropriate one would take time and tools he didn't have.

Ahead of him walls and windows were suddenly lit by a flash far brighter than the murky day. He looked back into the west, and saw there a cloud rising, an immense inverted cone of steam and spray, losing shape as the fire within it faded, dwarfing all the city's buildings. A hyperspace projectile had barely missed and had fallen into the ocean.

Moments later the ground jarred and shook with a force that flung Degnan to the pavement. He heard the tinkle of shattering glass and from somewhere the prolonged roar of collapsing structures. Dust and plaster fell from overhead. He scrambled to his feet and broke into a run again.

Three quarters of an hour later, spent from haste and from struggling through streets half-blocked with rubble, he reached his goal.

The small hotel looked deserted, though it was practically undamaged, having lost no more than a few windows. Degnan panted up the stairs—and paused in dismay; the door of the room where he had told Margaret to stay stood ajar.

As by its own will, his hand dipped into his pocket and came out with the pistol, slipped off the safety catch. Dead silence all around. He pushed the door wide with an abrupt motion, and looked into an empty room, almost as he had seen it last. A picture hanging askew, a lamp toppled—but that was no doubt caused by the temblors just past. Intuitively he knew she was gone, and at the same time his mind refused stupidly to grasp the possibility—gone without leaving any word? Or taken away?

Then a scuffing sound from behind warned him; he spun and recoiled inside the room, catching a flashing glimpse of the half-dozen men in police uniforms and civilian clothes who had appeared almost soundlessly. Degnan heaved a table against the door just as a crashing impact sprung the latch. A second blow jarred the heavy table back a couple of inches. Then Degnan took aim at the door, just above head level, and fired.

A sound of hasty steps and silence again, broken only by a mutter of voices in which he could catch no words.

He was in the bag. The room was on the third floor, and even so there'd be others posted around. This was the end...

"WHAT'S THE matter, Ralph? Can't we talk this over?"

Jay Marlin's voice from the hall outside. Degnan shifted his grip on the pistol butt, grown slippery in his hand. He answered in a flat voice, "No, I'm afraid not, Jay."

"Listen—we've got plenty of guns and gas out here, but we don't want to use either one. There are some who think the Venusians got to you, Ralph; but I don't believe it, I don't believe you'd turn against us. Whatever's happened, it can't be as important right now as a defense against the bombardment. And you're the only man that can give us that, the only man that can save Earth!"

How close that was to the truth and yet how grotesquely far away! He was not Earth's salvation but its greatest danger. Try to explain that? He remembered Athalie's unbelief and treachery. The chance was too great, the danger too monstrous. And yet—

He was silent, trying for a moment to put everything else out of his mind and look sanely, objectively at the thought that had come to him, trying to be sure it was not just that he was cracking up, his personal urge to cling to life getting the upper hand and urging him to grasp at a hope that was not there.

He said from a dry throat, "There was a girl here—"

"She's all right. We picked her up early this morning."

So Margaret had already been in their hands when her picture was broadcast. They would have suspected he might come back here, sent out the picture in hopes of increasing the probability. And they had guessed right, without knowing all that was at stake.

"Jay."

"Yes?"

"Maybe we can make a bargain."

"Name it..."

"I've got to have a solemn promise. Let me talk to that girl for a little while—half an hour. It doesn't have to be alone, just undisturbed. At the end of that time, I'll go quietly to CFHQ, unless—and you've got to promise me that, too— unless by then the bombardment has stopped."

There was a brief pause; then Jay Marlin said, "My word on that wouldn't do you much good. I'll have to call headquarters; that'll take a couple of minutes. These other men will stay right where they are. All right?"

"All right," said Degnan. He didn't move, but stood facing the door, the automatic in his hand.

After a lifetime, the other was there again. "Ralph—it's okay. I talked to General Fleming himself. He promises you'll be given what you ask."

Degnan let the gun fall; it thudded dully on the carpet. He pushed his barricade aside and let the door swing open.

IN THE anteroom of Fleming's office, Jay Marlin pressed his hand.

"Good luck. I don't know what you're trying to do, Ralph—but good luck anyway." He wheeled sharply, and went out before Degnan could manage so much as "Thanks."

There, thought Degnan, went a man who would have believed him.

Other NAMI agents accompanied Degnan into the office. The General was waiting, looking older than he had last night; with him was a youngish man with a smooth face and Mongoloid eyes.

"This is Mr. King," General Fleming waved a hand jerkily, "liaison deputy from Combined Fleet Headquarters. By his permission, we shan't have located you—officially—until thirty minutes from now."

King nodded and glanced silently at an expensive wristwatch.

Degnan hardy gave either of them a second look. He had eyes only for Margaret Lusk.

She was in a chair beside the General's big desk, and she looked very small and dejected. But at sight of Degnan she sprang to her feet with a tremulous glad cry.

"Ralph, Ralph!" She flung her arms about his neck. "They told me you'd disappeared—and I thought—"

"Easy," he said softly. "Things haven't gone just the way I figured, Margaret. I need your help again."

She raised her head and looked into his face clear-eyed. "Tell me how."

He couldn't believe, now, the dark suspicions that had burgeoned again not long ago—and that made what he had to ask harder. He steeled himself.

"Remember what you told me last night? About the thing that kept trying to creep back. Is it still trying?" A shadow of pain crossed the face close to his; she closed her eyes as if to shut something out.

"I think so—I'm afraid—"

"Stop being afraid—and let it come back and have control again just for a little while. You've built up a defense against it—you've got to tear the wall down now. It's the only thing that will help—and you're the only one that can do it." He was at once commanding and pleading.

She shuddered, then was quiet; but he could feel the effort she was making, the tenseness of her body. "I—I'll try."

GENTLY he seated her in the chair. She looked up at him for a long moment, then leaned back. After a little she closed her eyes, and he saw a wave of revulsion pass over her face. Her hands clenched in her lap and then slowly, deliberately unclasped. Her eyes stayed shut and she was still.

Degnan had to know how fast his time was passing. He glanced round and saw no clock, but his eye lit on King; he made a peremptory beckoning motion and pointed to his own wrist. The other man's slanted eyes read the gesture; face impassive, he unfastened his watch and handed it over.

Five, six minutes gone. "Margaret!"

Her eyes opened and stared; they were blank, blind, as they had been when he first looked into them on the *Sheneb*.

Degnan spoke to her, to the thing behind her eyes, slowly and distinctly. "I have twenty-four minutes left. When that time is up, unless by then the hyperspace bombardment has ceased and Venus is ready to surrender, I will be sent to Combined Fleet Headquarters. The Headquarters is located at the bottom of the Pacific Ocean." Out of the corner of his eye he saw the General and the liaison agent start and look at one another. He went on steadily, "Earth's oceans are water, hydrogen oxide. Their total mass is in the neighborhood of one and one-half quintillion tons, of which about one-tenth is hydrogen. One gram of hydrogen, converted into helium, yields seventeen hundred billion calories of heat…"

He added a few more rough calculations. The enemy could check and reduce them to exactitude in next to no time—if the message were heard, if the thing in Margaret's eye was not only here, in her mind, but also *there*, forty million miles away…

If they heard, and if they believed, it would take them time to decide—though far less time than men would have needed—and again time for radio signals to halt the hyperspace projectiles that were on their way to Earth now. And how long might it take for a thought to cross space? The speed of light—or less, or more? There was no way of knowing. The hands of King's watch moved at abnormal speed, as if the mechanism were running mad.

Degnan began again, repeated the message almost word for word, with slow deadly emphasis. It was as if his naked will strained to bridge the gulf of nothing and make contact with the enemy.

Venusians were not men. No man quite knew how they would respond to a given situation. He was offering them, now, the choice they had hurled at Earth: surrender or die. The people of Earth were willing to accept death before defeat. But the Over Race was coldly logical, and Degnan felt sure that it would not respond as man had done...

THERE was silence when he finished. And in the stillness the faint tintinnabulation of small objects in the room, responding to the Earth's ceaseless vibration beneath the onslaught it was enduring. The floor shook solidly, once or twice, at shock-waves from nearer hits.

Two-thirds of his time was gone. No use repeating the threat again—the battle was already lost or won.

Perhaps the Over Race could recognize one of their errors now—an oversight that was understandable, since Venus had no water and no oceans, and the chance of a sufficiently violent explosion under the pressure of a great mass of water inducing the hydrogen-helium reaction, by a star, must never have played much part in their thinking. But of course they knew the theoretical possibility, and that once begun in a hydrogen concentration vastly above that in the Sun, it would be a chain reaction. And they could figure the effects. Within minutes after the detonation of Earth's oceans, Venus too would be dead, sterilized by the terrific outrush of heat and radiation; it was doubtful if such a blast would leave any life in the Solar System. Watchers out in the Galaxy, if there were watchers, would record a *stella nova* of unaccountable briefness...

The other mistake the Venusians had made—the psychological one was probably a mystery to them even now.

Degnan called once more, "Margaret!"

She did not stir; she hardly seemed to breathe. He wanted urgently to see light in her eyes again, see her face alive once more, if so it be that this were the end. He grasped her shoulders and drew her erect, unresisting.

"Margaret—wake up. It's all over now." That was the truth, one way or another. "Come back to me, Margaret…" He bent to her parted lips. That seemed to rouse her; he felt her lips come alive under the kiss, and he felt her body lose its hypnotized rigidity.

He said close to her ear, "I'm sorry. I'm afraid I hurt you for nothing."

She sighed deeply. "I'm all right now. It's gone…and you're here…and I know it won't come back anymore," she murmured, like a little girl being comforted out of a nightmare.

General Fleming coughed. "Colonel Degnan. Your time is up."

DEGNAN released Margaret and turned away, his face a frozen mask. Did the Over Race's misunderstanding of human mentality go so far that they had imagined he was bluffing. Or had he misjudged the Over Race—were they too capable of the hatred stronger than death, which so often in the human past had led men to go to destruction, if only to take an enemy with them?

He said, "I'm ready," and to Margaret, "Don't worry. It won't be long."

But her face was stricken. She must have sensed something behind the words, or perhaps she remembered and understood something of the message he had tried to send.

Degnan didn't look at her again. The guards flanked him in the open doorway. The General said briskly, relievedly, "We've landed a flier in the street outside. Only a few minutes—"

King, seated on the edge of the General's desk and apparently absorbed in putting on his watch, looked up abruptly and said, "Wait." Fleming stared at him, opened his mouth; but the deputy from CFHQ gestured imperiously for silence.

Degnan tried to listen, and was hindered by a roaring in his ears. Unsteadily, he put a hand on the jamb of the door, and felt no vibration in the cool wood; and he saw the answer in the others' faces at the same time.

King reached for a phone at his elbow. "Sector Defense... That's right. Give me the Head Coordinator. At once." He snapped a curt question or two, listened, then broke the connection and asked for another, direct to Combined Fleet Headquarters. Waiting, he gazed quizzically at Degnan. "No projectiles have come in for close to three minutes now—and they were coming five or six to the minute. Now, what shall I tell the general staffs?"

General Fleming made an incoherent noise; his eyes darted from King to Degnan and then to Margaret, and his wrinkles, for perhaps the first time in their history, expressed something like fright. He looked on the verge of crossing himself.

Degnan moistened his lips. "They'd better get in touch with Venus right away and discuss surrender terms. The surrender of Venus, that is... The Over Race ought to agree in occupation and destruction of their spawning beds; it isn't in them to set their race above self-preservation. That way they'll be extinct after a generation; and we can get along with the Under Race."

Margaret moved quietly to Degnan's side, and he drew her against him; but he was bracing himself for the questions that would come as soon as King finished talking to CFHQ. He couldn't answer those questions—not until Earth ships had taken control on Venus and spiked the enemy's guns.

And then—

In him was still a cold, dead weight of knowledge: Venus was defeated, but the curse that had been laid on him remained. He was still and forever an outcast from the rest of his victorious kind...

Earth would be grateful; no doubt they would be ready to give anything he asked, perhaps even the right to remain among men. He couldn't do that, though.

Margaret nestled her head against his shoulder, and looked up with the beginning of a smile on her lips. She might smile again, in a world without fear, as she had in that picture on the telescreen... He blotted the thought out.

She said, "It's really over now, isn't it? And we're all right."

Degnan looked away for a moment. She was going to be hurt too, he realized, and the sooner it was over the better. For a moment, just now, he had wondered if she knew...

He said in a low voice, disjointedly, "The end of one thing is the beginning of another. Now that the System is safe for man—before long they'll he building the first ship to go beyond. A long trip, a one-way trip perhaps, for whoever's chosen to go. And I think—"

Her arm tightened about him in a close embrace of possession and understanding. She whispered: "As long as the starship will carry two..."

THE END

If you've enjoyed this book, you will not want to miss these terrific titles...

ARMCHAIR SCI-FI & HORROR DOUBLE NOVELS, $12.95 each

D-41   **FULL CYCLE** by Clifford D. Simak
IT WAS THE DAY OF THE ROBOT by Frank Belknap Long

D-42   **THIS CROWDED EARTH** by Robert Bloch
REIGN OF THE TELEPUPPETS by Daniel Galouye

D-43   **THE CRISPIN AFFAIR** by Jack Sharkey
THE RED HELL OF JUPITER by Paul Ernst

D-44   **WE THE MACHINE** by Gerald Vance
PLANET OF DREAD by Dwight V. Swain

D-45   **THE STAR HUNTER** by Edmond Hamilton
THE ALIEN by Raymond F. Jones

D-46   **WORLD OF IF** by Rog Phillips
SLAVE RAIDERS FROM MERCURY by Don Wilcox

D-47   **THE ULTIMATE PERIL** by Robert Abernathy
PLANET OF SHAME by Bruce Elliot

D-48   **THE FLYING EYES** by J. Hunter Holly
SOME FABULOUS YONDER by Phillip Jose Farmer

D-49   **THE COSMIC BUNGLARS** by Geoff St. Reynard
THE BUTTONED SKY by Geoff St. Reynard

D-50   **TYRANTS OF TIME** by Milton Lesser
PARIAH PLANET by Murray Leinster

ARMCHAIR SCIENCE FICTION CLASSICS, $12.95 each

C-13   **THE SUNKEN WORLD**
by Stanton A. Coblentz

C-14   **THE LAST VIAL**
by Sam McClatchie, M. D.

C-15   **WE WHO SURVIVED (THE FIFTH ICE AGE)**
by Sterling Noel

ARMCHAIR MASTERS OF SCIENCE FICTION SERIES, $16.95 each

MS-5   **MASTERS OF SCIENCE FICTION, Vol. Five**
Winston K. Marks—Test Colony and other tales

MS-6   **MASTERS OF SCIENCE FICTION, Vol. Six**
Fritz Leiber—Deadly Moon and other tales

THOU SHALT NOT COVET YOUR NEIGHBOR'S WIFE...OR EVEN YOUR OWN!

1000 years ago 30 men and 30 women were exiled from Earth to populate a recently discovered planet. In the ensuing years, the original groups' strict puritan beliefs (especially pertaining to <u>sex</u>) had become so overbearing, so warped in their nature, that the sexual practices of the culture (or the lack there of!) literally threatened the planet's populace with extinction.

The turning point came one night when a young man on a drunken bender (ordered by his own doctor no less!) began to question the logic of always living in such a loathsome and shameful state of mind.

With the help and encouragement from his new friends, John Comstock decides he really is willing to start a revolution of new ideas...and the public kissing of a young woman in the plaza was only the beginning of his rebellion!

CAST OF CHARACTERS

JAMES COMSTOCK
His entire world was turned upside down! Cowardice and bravery battled within him. Could he really be the unlikely hero?

DANNY GRUNDY
Befriending Comstock during a drunken aberrant moment helped set the wheels of rebellion in motion.

TONY BOWDLER
Mastermind behind the rebellion to overthrow "The Grandfather." Would his high ranking bureaucratic position be of any help?

HELEN
Young and attractive, she was the sexual catalyst for the exceedingly "dangerous" thoughts forming in Comstock's mind.

PAT MATHER
She was a fiery redhead ready to join the rebellion at any cost, even at the sacrifice of her own life…

THE PICAROON
This piratical nut-job was just what the rebels needed—a thieving madman who knew all the "ins and outs" of the night guards.

THE GRANDFATHER
Almost god-like, the idolized patriarch of the whole planet. What would it take to bring "Him" down, and what was his dark secret?

PLANET OF SHAME

By
BRUCE ELLIOTT

ARMCHAIR FICTION
PO Box 4369, Medford, Oregon 97504

Editor's Note:

In this novel, "Planet of Shame," you will notice words occasionally that are represented by the first letter of the word, followed by a series of periods—as though the words were censored. In this story about extreme morality, we believe it may have been the author's intention to "suppress" certain words that might have been deemed "objectionable" within the morals and culture of the fictional planet represented in the story. We have left these intact.

Greg Luce,
Editor-in-Chief,
Armchair Fiction

AT THE END...

"THE THREE who had endured so much sat and waited. Their reward was in sight. When you have fought for so long against forces strong beyond imagining, when you have struggled in despair, lived without hope, success when it finally comes, is almost anti-climactic. Despite the traps, the violence, the hurts, the fear, they were now where they had wanted to be.

They sat quietly, their hands folded, and if any feeling of triumph was in them, it was so muted as not to be observable. At that precise moment, when they sat in the anteroom, waiting for their reward, waiting to become part of the Board of Fathers, working directly under The Grandfather, the only common emotion they shared was that they had fought the good fight. Fought as hard as it is in a person to fight for what they consider right...

The door opened and The Grandfather was in the room. His visage was marked by a high hooked nose, broad high forehead, and deep set harsh blue eyes, focused on the middle distance. His strong old hands were crossed on his stomach just below his patriarchal beard.

It was hard to believe.

Hard to believe that they, or anyone below the rank of Father would ever actually behold Him in the flesh.

When he spoke his voice was all the things they had known it would be. Deep as an organ bass, calm, full of authority, stern yet with a leavening of those other things that make up the whole man, his voice was almost gentle as he said, "Follow me, please."

They rose and feeling like children, followed his tall spare back out of the anteroom, into that other room where the Board waited for them.

There was no fear in them now as there would have been a year ago. For they were not coming before the Board for judgment, but to be rewarded.

The Grandfather said, "These three are the ones…"

There was silence.

"They have come to join us," The Grandfather said.

The silence expanded.

"Gentlemen, Fathers all, these are the three new Fathers." The Grandfather's voice faded away and there was no other sound. None of the ten men who made up the Board of Fathers said a word.

But the three who had fought their way up to this eminence stood in silence and looking about them, examined the ten men with whom they would now share the control of their whole world.

This was the moment of their triumph.

CHAPTER ONE

WHEN the first spaceship landed on that pleasant world (the only pleasant planet of which Alpha Centauri could boast) the crew was so happy to get rid of the passengers that they took off the moment they could. Not even the interminable boredom of the return trip was enough to make them want to stay in anything like proximity with the thirty men and thirty women who had been sentenced to be marooned as far from earth as was humanly possibly.

There had been maximum-security prisons in the past. But this was the ultimate maximum. When the ship took off, the prisoners were isolated as no human beings ever had been in the recorded history of men.

It was part of a plan of course. Earth did want the planet inhabited just as earlier powers had wanted Mars colonized. But when no volunteers appeared despite the cleverest high pressure advertising campaigns, the alternative became clear. If no one wanted to go to the new planet, to New Australia, then someone would have to be forced to go there.

It was just too bad for the exiles, but they could not protest too loudly, since they had long since forfeited any claim on anyone's sympathy. A little back eddy of intransigent inner-directed people, fanatics in a world of other-directed humans, positive that they, and they alone knew what was good and what was evil; the world heaved a communal sigh of relief when they were taken away. Attempting, as these sixty had, to turn back the clock, to bring back into being the dark days of the twenty-second century, was such a horrid crime as to merit even so harsh a sentence as they received.

The first hundred and fifty years on New Australia were, in a way difficult. But not too difficult. To these inner-directed people fighting for existence on a new planet was precisely the kind of crusade, which to them was worth living.

Five hundred years after they established themselves, their last scientist managed to set up a system of protective devices which prevented any communication with Mother Earth at all. No earth ship landed or took off, and no other means of communication had yet been devised that would work in interstellar space.

A thousand years later even the memory of earth had faded and grown dim. There were mentions of it of course in old books, but they were not the kind of books that these people read.

Their sun rose and set, their erratic moon rose when it seemed to feel like it and sank seemingly just as randomly, their days were full and to them worth living.

All sixty of the first settlers had married. Sixty humans, thirty family names. They were, to these people good names, and therefore there had never been felt any need for new patronymics.

The planet's sprawling surface now contained millions of people but all of them shared thirty last names. It was nothing for anyone to question since to them this had always been the case. Science as such was an unknown word. It was one of the things that the original sixty settlers had fought against. When they made their brave new world, science was one of the earth things that was jettisoned. This, of course, led to some strange circumstances...

James Comstock 101, had reached maturity. At thirty-five he felt that the time had come for him to leave the home nest and go out on his own. His mother, as was to be expected, fought against his plans. But dad came through, as good old dad would.

Dad had said, "Now mother, admittedly Jimmy is still a little boy, but even little boys have a right to strike out for themselves."

"But Father," mother only called him that when something serious was under discussion, for after all, "Father" was a term of...Jimmy didn't know quite what to think of it as...power? Awe? It was, in any event a word that one did not bandy about.

"But Father," mother had become embarrassed, and surely that was a blush on her cheeks, "did you...have you ever... that is...what about...oh, you know."

Father had looked very serious. He had said, his voice deep in his chest, "You're right, of course. Come, son."

Then had come that conversation, which had stunned Jimmy, opened up vistas unheard of, unthought of, really. So that was where babies came from… If anyone but his Father had told him about it he'd have struck them, perhaps killed them. To think that his mother had suffered through such an abysmal, horrible experience…and the results of that experience… Tremors swept through him in retrospect.

But that had been five years previously and Jimmy had become a man then under his father's aegis. That first time had been cataclysmically awful. The whole atmosphere of that place had been so foreign to him that it was only because he knew that his father was waiting downstairs in the parlor, waiting for a good report from the fallen woman that enabled Jimmy to go through with it at all. Not that the woman had waxed very enthusiastic, but then, a creature like that…

HIS monthly visits to the brothel were now part of his being and although he still did not relish going, he forced himself to, for after all it was part of the duty of a man. He did so wish, however, that it was not necessary. Life would be so much simpler if he could just skip the whole unsavory thing.

Sighing, he pressed the button on the door. Inside the curtained window the brash lights of the place, red as sin, shone on his weakly handsome face. The tinkle of the piano droned on.

Swinging the door wide, the fat Madame said jovially, "Jimmy my boy. Come on in and let joy be unrefined."

Shuddering delicately and wishing that the Madame would not be quite so robust, Jimmy inched his way into the parlor. The red plush chairs and the dingy lights were just as they always were. At the piano the little man looked up, said, "Hi ya, Jimmy, how's every little thing?"

"Pretty good, professor, pretty good." The whole conversation was as stereotyped as the act, which would follow it. Sometimes Jimmy wished that just once the Madame would sneer at him, or the professor be grouchy, but they never were.

Lydia came down the stairs, her wrapper as dirty and unkempt as it always was. He wondered if she had a succession of these wrappers all equally dilapidated, or if she owned just one which she managed to keep looking the same way all the time.

Jimmy wished too, that Lydia were a little older. It seemed somehow a little indecent for her to be only forty. A child like that should not be forced to make a living the way she had to, but then they were all about her age. Jimmy had shopped around, tried to find an older woman but had been forced back into Lydia's arms. After all, she had been the one Father selected for him and good old dad knew best.

She said, "Come on upstairs honey lamb."

He followed her dolefully, averting his eyes from her full breasts which was altogether too prominent through the tight cloth of the wrapper.

Her room looked as if it had not been cleaned since the previous month. Stuck to the mirror was the picture of The Grandfather that always embarrassed him. The stern old eyes should not be forced to look down on the scenes in this room. Jimmy had tried to turn the picture to the wall one time, but Lydia had become hysterical and he had given up. As a matter of fact it was only after a long argument and an increase in fee that Jimmy had been able to force her to turn out the light in the room when they did what they did.

The old brass bed jingled just as embarrassingly as ever when he sat down on the edge of it to remove his shoes. It was only by keeping his eyes on his stockinged feet that he was able to avoid looking at Lydia who had dropped her wrapper to the floor and was now shamelessly considering herself in front of the mirror that lined the whole wall.

That had been the main reason he had insisted on the light being extinguished. The combination of the wall of mirror, the ceiling mirror and the searching eyes of The Grandfather were just more than he could bear.

There was no use, he knew, in asking Lydia not to look at her n..e body. She had told him many times that she enjoyed doing it; there was no law against it and what was he going to do about it?

Of course there *was* a law against women admiring themselves in any way, let alone n..e and in front of a mirror, but the law, of course, did not apply to p.........s.

Whistling gaily, Lydia dropped onto the bed next to him and wound her arms about him.

Almost dying with embarrassment he mumbled, "Lydia, the light…you promised."

Grumbling, she switched off the light. Then it began, again.

But this time, right in the middle, a lancing pain unlike anything he had ever experienced shot through his heart. The hurt was so great that he cried out in agony.

Lydia, unknowing, said cheerfully, "Attaboy. That's what I like to hear."

It was only after he gasped, "Don't…stop…my heart…I think I'm going to die…" that she finally stopped and turned on the light. His face was whiter, much whiter than the grey pillowcase under his head. His lips were purple. He still felt what he could only visualize as iron fingers pressing into his heart.

Racing out of bed the girl ran towards the door. She gasped. "I'll call the Madame, get a doctor…"

Crouched on the bed in agony, his hand pressing deep into the center of the pain, he was still able to retain the presence of mind to call weakly, "Put on your wrapper, Lydia, you can't go out that way."

Then the pain became so great that he passed out.

WHEN he opened his eyes he was in bed but it was another bed, with crisp white linen on it. The pain, he was grateful to find, had eased up.

The adult woman in the nurse's uniform, who must have been a pleasant sixty-five, bent over him and whispered, "There, there, you'll feel much better now."

"The doctor?" he whispered.

"Coming." Her sweet face was wreathed in an angelic smile. Her buxom body was omnipresent. Wondering what kind of perverted monster he was, he found that he was fantasying her in Lydia's bed. If only fallen women were mature, like this one, so many of his problems would be easier of solution. He guessed he just did not like young chits and that was all there was to it.

Luckily the doctor entered the room before the fantasy could go too far. Feeling mentally defiled, he greeted the doctor anxiously, glad of the interruption. "Doctor, do you know what's wrong with me?"

"Yes son," the white-haired elderly man was slow of speech, he considered each syllable before he allowed it to leave his thin lips. His sunken cheeks and hollow eyes were so typical of the whole medical profession that Jimmy found himself wondering, as he had before, what there was about doctoring that made men look like this.

"What do I have, doctor?" Jimmy's voice was tremulous.

"I've got bad news for you, son." It must have taken three minutes for the single sentence to be articulated by the doctor.

Sweating, Jimmy wondered what he had ever done, what commandment he could have unconsciously broken that was now punishing him for his sin.

"What is the cure, doctor?"

"First," the doctor said, "we must consider the disease."

Jimmy wasn't the least bit interested in what disease he had, there were cures for all known diseases. But he waited with baited breath to be told what terrible, what terrifying thing he would have to do in order to be cured.

"You have," the doctor said even more slowly, "angina pectoris."

Scrambling through his memory, Jimmy tried to remember what heart patients had to do. All he could think of at the moment was the treatment for arterio-sclerosis. It was so awful that he found himself saying a little prayer of thankfulness to The Grandfather, that he did not have to indulge in that cure. Adultery was the only known cure for hardening of the arteries and the prospect of what he would have had to go through made Jimmy almost glad that he had angina. Imagine, he kept thinking, "I'd have had to get married and then be untrue to my wife…"

His gratitude faded a little when the doctor's droning voice went on, "As you may or may not know, son, the only cure for what you've got is drunkenness. We'll have to make you into an alcoholic, boy. I'm sorry."

The world reeled.

Jimmy had seen drunks, who hadn't, but the thought of having to share their disgraceful conduct was more than he could bear. He gasped, "I won't do it. I'd rather die."

"Umm…" the doctor said, "a lot of them say that…but remember, boy, suicide is what you're talking about!"

Suicide, Jimmy thought sickly, the sin against The Grandfather!

Horrible as the cure for his disease was, he'd have to go through with it. But what would mother think when he came reeling home, singing songs, consorting with…he retched, no more seeing Lydia once a month, he'd have to consort with fallen women all the time…

Thank Grandfather, he thought dully, that dad is dead. It was the only thing for which he could feel grateful at the moment.

"Cheer up," the grey-faced doctor said and his voice was if anything more doleful than before, "be grateful you don't have cancer."

That was another thing for which to be grateful. The cure for cancer was the only thing he had ever heard of that was more horrible than that awful cure for arterio-sclerosis.

"Of course," the doctor said, "before we release you, we'll test you for all the known diseases."

Grandfather above, he thought despairingly, suppose something else is wrong with me!

CHAPTER TWO

HIS heart condition was all the doctor found. Jimmy thought the medical man was a little grudging in the admission that nothing else was discernibly wrong, but gratitude that he was not worse off made him feel a little better.

Leaving the hospital with the lovely, elderly nurse holding him by one arm, and the doctor on the other side of him, Jimmy looked around him, at the street, at the people, at the mauve trees with their lovely puce foliage. It was night and the pale green moon moving in its eccentric path cast just the faintest tone over the whole scene. Admirably dressed women, their beautiful shapeless clothes hanging loosely so that nothing of their bodily contours could be seen, walked sedately along the black plastic street, their dresses barely avoiding dragging on the eternal surface with which the last scientists, so many years ago, had covered the roads and the streets.

Perpetua, it was called, and seemingly it was correctly named. Striving madly to forget that which awaited him, Jimmy thought wildly about the street covering, about, in short, everything but the saloon that he was being escorted to…would the doctor and the nurse take him through the swinging doors? Or would he have to make that brave first step all by himself?

The doctor cleared his throat. "We're almost there, son. Be brave."

Be brave? A fine thing to say. It was easy for the doctor to make speeches, but he, Jimmy Comstock 101, was the one who was going to have to enter the foul place!

And then, despite the slowness of his steps, they were finally there. He realized, looking at the saloon that he had never really looked at one of these dens of iniquity before. He had always, in the past, gone by them with averted eyes.

He reeled, and the lovely nurse, her exquisitely wrinkled face showing her concern, grabbed at him just in time to prevent him from falling to his face.

"There, there, Jimmy boy," her cracked voice was so…soothing and at the same time so exciting…he found himself beginning to fantasy about her again, and it was only this that gave him the bravado necessary to step through the swinging door.

A gust of beery air hit him in the voice. His throat closed up in revulsion at the disgusting odor. Behind him he could hear the nurse say, "Grandfather be with you now!"

And then she and the doctor were gone, and he was alone. Alone in the moiling turmoil, the frightful, frightening atmosphere of that which he must become. To the right, the left, everywhere he looked there were fellow heart disease patients. All of them were treating their disease. Some seriously, some seeming even to enjoy it, which Jimmy found impossible of comprehension. One of the ones who seemed to be enjoying the treatment of his disease staggered up to him with a fog of alcohol preceding him.

"Hi chum!" The drunk was small and young and seemingly very happy.

Jimmy gulped. "Hello, there, how are you? I'm James Comstock 101. Who are you?"

"Danny Grundy 112. C'mon kiddo, wancha to meet an old buddy of mine."

The drunk had him by the arm and there was no escape. Grundy pulled him through the welter of men and women who lined the bar and gulped or sipped their poisonous yet beneficial potions.

Behind the bar a tremendously fat man, a white apron pulled tight around the huge circumference of what Jimmy thought of as his tummy, said, "What'll it be? What's your pleasure?"

Jimmy turned to his newfound friend and asked, "How can I get drunk the fastest, easiest way?"

"Leave it to me, old buddy, old sock," Grundy said.

"Maxwell, mix up three of your super-double extra strong corpse revivers, will you like a pal?"

"Surest thing you know." Max busied himself with bottles containing oddly colored liquors.

Rather than look at the terrible thing he was going to have to drink, Jimmy asked, "Where is the man you wanted me to meet?"

A howl of laughter from a nearby group drowned out his words, forcing him to repeat himself. Grundy looked at the group and said, "There he is. I'll bring him over."

The man he dragged to meet Comstock was equally young, no more than thirty-eight, with an unformed face, and the barest amount of white hair at the temples. He had some pictures in his hand and as he was introduced to Jimmy he held out the photos.

Grundy said, "Tony Bowdler 131, wancha to meet my oldest friend, Jimmy—what was your name, old sock?"

Jimmy identified himself and as he turned his eyes to look at the pictures, Bowdler mumbled, "Do' wancha to think I'm unner the affluence of inkohol, but lemme know how you like them feelthy pictures."

The man's voice was blurred and Jimmy could not quite comprehend what he was saying. That was the only reason he looked at the top picture. All the blood drained out of his head. There, on the picture, brazenly posed for anyone to see, were a man and a woman. Good looking people too. The woman was real s..y. Almost seventy, with exciting white hair, and a deeply wrinkled face, she was even more desirable than the nurse.

How then had she ever allowed a despicable picture like this one to be taken? It was beyond Jimmy, completely beyond him. Frozen in the glossy eternity of the picture, her loose dress lifted so that her ankle showed, she was allowing the man in the picture to k..s her hand.

The picture blurred in front of Jimmy's dazed eyes. This was a kind of perversion beyond his reckoning. How could people allow such a thing?

Grundy said, "You think that's hot, boy, lay a glim on some of the others! Here, look at these," he spread them out one at a time and giggled inanely. "This last picture is a real killer! Take a peak!"

Comstock shook his head no, but his new found friend paid no attention to him. Pointing to the foul pictures lined up on the bar he picked up the last one and held it right under Jimmy's nose. Just before he forced his eyes closed, the picture was engraved on his sickened brain.

The people were the same as the ones in the other picture, but, oh the depth of depravity, oh poor lost souls, the man was actually k…ing the woman full on the m…h!

The bartender said, "Hey, what's wrong with the Johnny-come-lately? Looks like he's going to faint. Better get some medicine in him fast!"

Bowdler grabbed Jimmy's one arm, Grundy the other, while the stout bartender poured the drink down Comstock's slack mouth. Gagging, half-spitting, he still swallowed enough so that he could feel what he thought was liquid fire going down his aching throat.

"How's that feel, ol' pal?" Bowdler asked anxiously.

"Awful," Jimmy said, but he sipped more of it anyhow. This was his curse, this was his cure, he had to take it, so he took it.

THE bartender went back to his other customers, and the trio raised their glasses. Jimmy's newfound friends were teaching him how to make a toast.

"Here's to heart trouble," Grundy said, "thank Grandfather I didn't get cancer!"

"Tha's the boy. Drink her down… Bottoms up…" Bowdler put his hand over his mouth. "Mus' 'pologize," he said, "reelize don't know you well enough to talk that way. Ve'y sorry, ole man."

Comstock gagged again, but this time not from the drink, but as a conditioned reflex. At that moment he could again taste the soap his mother had used to wash out his mouth that time when he was but a lad of twenty-nine, and he had slipped and said something about the b....m of a well. The drink helped to wash out the long enduring soap taste.

"Yeah," Grundy was saying. "I don't care how drunk a man gets, a gentleman never uses dirty words."

"You're righ' ole pal, ole pal. I'm sorry..." Bowdler hung his head in shame. As though to change the subject he picked up his pornographic pictures and looked through them lovingly. At last, pausing over one that Comstock could see showed a man and woman in the last stages of reckless abandon, (they were holding hands) Bowdler said, "Y' know if I din' like gettin' drunk so much I'd be sorry I din't have tuberculosis so I could pose for feelthy pix like these."

"Y' know," Grundy had his arm wrapped lovingly around Jimmy's neck by now and they were on their second set of corpse revivers, "y' know I've known fallen women who told me they were kina glad they had diabetes. Don't seem possible, does it?"

"No." Jimmy's face was set sternly. "I cannot imagine snuch a ting. I mean I cannot magine uch a sting..." He rubbed his mouth. It felt a little strange.

Bowdler ordered another round. Nearby a particularly abandoned looking woman who must have been in the last stages of coronary thrombosis if the amount of liquor she had imbibed was any indication, waved to Jimmy.

He turned his head away quickly, hoping no one else had seen what the woman did. He was instantly sorry he had done so for suddenly the room swirled.

When it stopped, he turned to Grundy and said, "Shay, how offen doesa room do that?"

"Do what?" Grundy asked, his mouth slack.

"How offen do they make it go roun' and roun' like that?"

Evidently he had said something highly amusing for his new friends went off in gales of laughter. They had to whack each other on the back before they could make their giggles subside.

Grundy said, finally, "If you think this room is movin' wait'll you see your bedroom move tomorrow morning!" Then he and Bowdler went off into helpless laughter again.

Comstock tried to explain that there was no special mechanism in his room, which would allow it to spin in any fashion at all, but the combination of the peculiar trouble he was having in articulating and the roars of laughter from Bowdler and Grundy made him finally desist. Perhaps this was some joke that he would have explained at some future time.

The fourth drink, Comstock found must have had some different ingredients in it although he had watched the bartender carefully and seemingly the same constituents went into the making of it, but, on sipping it, he found that the taste was different. He no longer felt as if he was going to die in agony when he swallowed. Instead, a rather pleasant kind of warmth went all through him.

He gazed at his new friends. New? How dare he consider them that? These were his pals. Why...he'd cut off his right arm for either of them.

He felt a desire to explain this sudden feeling of camaraderie, but that odd thing affected his speech again and the words did not come out quite as he had expected they would. He wondered if a stutter or a stammer was part of angina pectoris, but that did not seem likely somehow.

The sixth drink he never had any remembrance of downing. As a matter of fact, the following morning when he woke up he had all he could do to figure out how, when and who had installed the merry-go-round mechanism in his room. Apparently the saloon was not the only place so equipped. Lying in bed, looking about him, he at first wondered if he were in some strange place, but second thought reassured him. He was home, in his own bed. The colored portrait of Grandfather looked down at him...he hoped that the picture did not reflect any disapproval on Grandfather's part. He mumbled, "I can't help it... I'm sick...the doctor made me..."

Then he held onto the sides of the bed for dear life and prayed that whoever was making the room turn around would stop sooner or later, preferably sooner.

On one of the circling trips the room seemed to slow down a tiny bit and he was able to crawl out of bed onto the floor. The floor was bigger and he lost the fear he had had in bed that he was going to fall out. At least there was no place to fall now.

When his mother entered the room he was curled up peacefully on the rug, sound asleep.

She woke him gently and gave him a glass of milk.

Jimmy eyed his mother in horror. How could he ever have loved a woman who could do such a terrible thing? The milk seemed to be fastened directly to his stomach. Racing from the room he found that there are more than a few problems connected with being a drunk.

WHEN he came back and fell into his bed, his mother moved around the room, opening the curtains letting in the sunlight, as she had every day of his life.

He said, "Mother, will you please take those hobnails out of your shoes? And whatever you're doing to those curtains, stop it. The racket's enough to rouse the dead."

"They wouldn't let me come to the hospital, dear," she said. "Was it very bad for my little boy?"

"Very bad. Did you get the report on me?"

She nodded. "But do I really have to give you that poison they recommended for your mornings?"

"What poison?" If she'd only stop yelling.

"Coffee…"

At that moment he knew he would have sold his soul for a cup of coffee. Aloud he said, "Bring it…fast! And get that sickening glass of milk out of here. It's leering at me."

Shaking her head, she left.

If the inside sweats would only stop a moment, he thought, he'd be able to take time out to feel sorry for her. After all she hadn't raised her son to be a drunkard…it must be very difficult for her. But a question rose large in his mind. How had those bats gotten into his insides? Looking down at it, feeling what the bats were doing to the wall of his stomach, he called it a belly for the first time in his life.

"My belly," he said to himself, "hurts." And he didn't even feel the soap sensation in his mouth. But then the taste that was already there was so much like the inside of a parrot's cage that perhaps the psychic soap was just lost in the other, more horrible, taste.

Curiously he found that the steaming, jet black coffee made him feel better. How had he known it would? Perhaps Grundy...or Bowdler had told him about it...

His mother watched him drink the dread potion silently. Then she said, "My poor, poor boy. When do you have to do this terrible thing again?"

He lifted his head just a little and found that he could endure the sunlight. In some lost cavern in the back of his head he heard Bowdler's drunken voice saying, "And if you think you're gonna die, buddy boy, remember, a hair of the dog will fix you up."

The idea of eating a dog's hair almost made him run for the bathroom again, but he conquered the feeling.

Then he considered his mother's question. When must he get drunk again? Why...right now. This minute. Besides, he wanted to find out more about these puzzles that baffled him from his buddies. He smiled remembering the good feeling of fellowship that had been his when he had sung some old song with Bowdler and Grundy.

How did the words go?

His startled mother raised her eyebrows when her poor sick boy lurched to the side of his bed and began to hum, "For he's a jolly good fellow..."

Yep.

Back to the saloon.

That's where he belonged.

Rising slowly from some subterranean depth was the dawning realization that he was beginning to enjoy his ailment...

Good old Grundy...Good old Bowdler...they were indeed the salt of the planet.

CHAPTER THREE

THE portions of a woman's anatomy,'" Grundy was singing when Jimmy entered the bar, "'that appeal to man's depravity, are fashioned with considerable care...'" He broke off his song when he saw Comstock.

"Buddy boy!"

Bowdler rushed over and threw his arms around Jimmy, "How's the old kid?"

"Fine, just fine. How about a drink?" Comstock found himself asking, just as though he'd been a barroom habitué all his life.

The corpse revivers served their functions admirably, Jimmy found. In fact in just short of an hour, he was high on a cloud, feeling no pain.

That was when Grundy, whom Jimmy had thought was quite drunk, had drawn Bowdler and Comstock to a quiet table in the back of the saloon. Carrying their drinks they joined him. Jimmy was puzzled, for suddenly Grundy had become very serious. Bowdler seemed to know what was in the wind.

When they were seated comfortably and Jimmy was sipping happily at his drink, Grundy looked around conspiratorially before he whispered, "Jimmy, how old is The Grandfather?"

The question was a double shocker. First because Jimmy was positive that this was the first time that holy name had ever been mentioned in such unhallowed precincts, and second because the veriest infant knew the answer. He said, "The Grandfather was, is and always will be."

Grundy grinned. "How do you know that to be true?"

Comstock's world stopped spinning. His breath froze in his lungs. Then he felt a heart attack coming on. He fell face forward onto the floor.

Bowdler said, "Now see what you've done! You should have led up to it more gradually."

"Let's see if we can revive him," Grundy's normally jolly face was set and strained.

When Comstock opened his eyes and felt consciousness return he found that his friends had him propped up in his chair and were pouring liquor down his throat. Gasping, he spluttered, "All right, all right. I'm okay now."

There was a pause, then Comstock asked, "What happened to me?"

The two other men avoided his eyes. Bowdler said at long last, "I guess you're not quite drunk enough."

He ordered another round of drinks and as they waited for the elderly waitress to bring them to the table Jimmy found himself remembering what had happened.

The only thing that prevented his passing out again was that the s..y waitress returned with their corpse revivers. He took a big slug, considered her bent back as she walked away and said, "I...seem to remember your asking me something about..."

"I did." Grundy's face was set with determination. "Now hold onto yourself, laddy boy. How do you know that The Grandfather has always been and always will be?"

The traumatic shock was strong again but he had drunk some more and so was able to hold on while all the blood drained out of his head. He finally managed to say weakly, "Because everyone knows that to be true." Life without Grandfather was inconceivable. Who would look after them? Protect them? To whom could a man turn if not to The Grandfather?

Grundy and Bowdler exchanged meaningful glances. "If He always was, how come there's no record of His having made the trip from Earth?"

A trifle drunkenly, Comstock considered the question. Earth? Oh, yes that was the fable, the children's tale that his people had emigrated from some other planet. He had dismissed the whole thing as the usual kind of Father Goose story that kiddies were told. Aloud he asked, "You mean you two think there really is another inhabited planet?"

"Think?" Both men spoke simultaneously, but it was Grundy who continued, "We know it. Look, Jimmy, we're risking a great deal, and before we go on, we'll have to swear you to secrecy. Whether you join us in what we have in mind, or not, you must swear on your father's memory that you will be silent as the grave..."

They waited, poised on the edge of their chairs with nervousness.

When he deliberated so long that their nerves were jangling, Bowdler said, "Look, Jimmy, do you want to have to live and die as a drunk, just because it's the only known cure for your disease?"

Things were popping too fast for Comstock to be able to grapple with them intelligently. He mumbled, "Nothin' wrong with being a drunk. I like it fine."

Grundy sprang to the attack. "That's too bad, old man, because it means the cure won't work. You should know that, the doc should have told you! The vice must be distasteful or the cure doesn't work!"

Looking back on the Comstock of yesterday, Jimmy could see why the doctor had not felt it necessary to make this point. It certainly had been unpredictable that he'd enjoy drinking. But it was his new friends who had made it fun... Had they done it deliberately? Too much to grapple with...he'd better wait and see what they had in mind. He said, "I swear to keep silent."

Bowdler said, "Go ahead, Grundy, it's your story."

Parenthetically, he explained to Jimmy, "You know, or I guess maybe you don't, that before Bowdler here, got sick, he was Head Genealogist."

"No kidding!" Comstock was amazed. Head Genealogist! Whew...that was a post that almost ranked with being a Father. Bowdler was...or had been, a big man!

"As part of my job," Bowdler said, "I went back to the beginning. I checked the passenger list on the Bon Aventure, the spaceship that brought the original Thirty to this planet from Earth."

Gulping down his drink hurriedly Comstock ordered another round. To mention the Thirty...it was *almost* as blasphemous as talking about The Grandfather. These two were dangerous men. He'd listen to what they said, but then he must, literally *must*, report them to the authorities! He was sorry for them for he liked them, but blasphemy like this had to be punished.

Bowdler went on, "That was the first time the thought occurred to me to wonder about ole Grandpop!"

Grandpop? Blasphemy piled on blasphemy. Comstock could feel his ears burning.

"And you know something," Bowdler lowered his voice to the veriest whisper of communicable sound, "There was no record of His having made the trip. None at all."

THE silence dragged itself out. Comstock was in a condition bordering on insanity. Although he managed to keep his face still. The temerity of these two...apostates!

"As a matter of cold brutal fact," Bowdler said broodingly, "there is no record of The Grandfather at all until about five hundred years ago. I checked, I read books that no one, absolutely no one, has even looked at for centuries...and by Grandpop himself, there's not even a mention of Him, till about a hundred years after they killed off the last scientists."

No one had ever before discussed these things openly, or covertly, with Comstock. A new emotion was beginning to make itself felt. He was becoming interested. The last scientists...he remembered all about them from school. The monsters. It was a good thing they had been wiped out. But even so it was exciting hearing it talked about. He leaned forward on the table and sipped his drink more slowly. There was plenty of time to report Bowdler and Grundy. After all, the authorities would want as much information as he could get.

Grundy spoke for the first time in a long time. He said, "That's where I come in. I used to be custodian of the hall of records."

Jimmy felt a little better. After all, a janitor! His job before he'd become ill had been better than that. He had been a law clerk at the Bureau of Commandments...it didn't compare with the office that Bowdler had held, and yet it was certainly a lot better than... But Grundy was speaking. He said, "Bowdler got his heart attack when he began to wonder about where The Grandfather had come from. I got mine when I was ordered by the Board of Fathers..."

"Oops," Comstock thought, a janitor working for the Fathers was nothing to be sneezed at, he'd better wait and see what was coming.

Grundy went on, "The only reason I even looked at the record I was supposed to burn was because I had glanced at it and had seen a G. I wondered if it had something to do with my family..." He put his hands to his forehead. "If only I hadn't... I'd still be happily at work...with no heart trouble...and with no need to drink this stuff..." He gulped down some of his drink.

"Buck up, old man," Bowdler said. "What's done is done."

"You're right. I must be a man." He shook his head dolefully. "It wasn't about my family at all. It was about the Gantrys...and you know how powerful that bloodline is. I don't have to tell you. Ever since Elmer the First, they've been on top of the heap."

Comstock nodded. As if any sane person would even question the qualifications of the Gantrys to be leaders? These two men were even more dangerous than he had suspected. It was up to him to keep his mouth shut and his ears open, by The Grandfather it was!

The furrows in Grundy's forehead were deeper now. His elbows on the table, his head in his hands, he looked off into the middle distance. He said, and he was almost speaking to himself, his voice was so low, "It was only when I examined the records that I began to wonder if it was truly ordained that the Gantrys were the leaders and would be the leaders, under The Grandfather's eagle eye. Funny," he mused, "all it takes is the tiniest notion to question these eternal verities, and then without your even being aware of it, the questions begin to demand answers…"

Bowdler broke in. "That was the mood Grundy was in when he and I met here in the saloon. Two men, both possessed of a tiny bit of knowledge not shared by anyone else on New Australia, and by chance we met here…"

Jimmy drained his glass and the action of tilting his head back brought the level of his eyes higher than it had been. That was the only reason he saw the face that was framed in a little window at the back of the barroom.

His breath shot out of his lungs as though he had been hit by the hind legs of an astrobat. He gulped, "Grundy! Bowdler!"

Their heads swiveled and they too saw what had frightened him.

"One of the Father's Right Arms," Bowdler said. Then, with a visible attempt to keep his voice down and his face from showing the fear that gripped all three of them, he said, "This is what we had to be prepared for; are you with us, Comstock?"

Now was the moment for decision. If, Jimmy thought, he were to act bravely, throw himself on the two apostates and wait for the R.A. to get to them, he could then explain what horrors the two evil men had been discussing. But, and the canker of indecision gnawed at him, but, what after all had he really learned? Only that these two men were questioning the eternal verities. There was more to it, much more, of that he was convinced.

There was perhaps an inch of liquor left in Jimmy's glass. Draining it, he made the decision, which he was instantly to regret. He said, "I'm with you two. What shall we do?" Better, he had decided, to go along with Grundy and Bowdler and pretend to be part of their horrid scheme, which was the only way that later on he could report fully to the Fathers.

Grundy and Bowdler smiled at each other. Grundy said, "He's with us. Let's go."

All this time the R.A. had been watching them, his little eyes preternaturally alert, his gaunt hand steadily holding the gun that pointed straight at them, his attention completely focused on the trio.

Bowdler leaned forward on the table till his head was close to Jimmy's. He whispered, "When I say three, duck to the floor. Stay there till I grab you."

All around the three men the life of the saloon went on blithely. The other heart disease patients were drinking; some solemnly, some gaily, the aged waitresses were busy with their Hebe-like duties, the bartenders were mixing drinks, but to Jimmy, the whole of life...and perhaps death were contingent upon the next three seconds.

"One," Bowdler's voice whispered.

Jimmy could see Grundy bunching his heavy muscles for some kind of action.

"Two."

Watching the R.A. out of the corner of his eyes, Jimmy wondered if it was just his imagination or if he had really seen the R.A.'s trigger finger tighten on the stun gun's trigger.

"Three!"

CHAPTER FOUR

LATER, looking back on the scene that followed, Jimmy was never quite sure just what had happened in just what order. For the first thing that erupted was the table. Grundy had suddenly tilted back in his chair throwing his heavy body over backwards.

His legs, under the table, served to catapult the heavy object straight up towards the little spy window where the R.A. waited.

Bowdler had thrown his own empty glass straight at the eternally lit little bulb that had supplied the only illumination.

Darkness, then the crash of the table, then Comstock had obeyed orders and thrown himself flat on the floor. Next to him he had heard Bowdler land heavily.

The second crash as the table fell to the floor was the signal for Bowdler to grab Comstock by the arm and whisper, "Crawl after me."

Darkness and silence.

None of the other heart patients in the saloon had uttered a sound. That was not surprising of course, as anything unusual that ever happened was always the result of the action of the R.A.'s and it ill behooved anyone to interfere with them…

The only sign of light was the little flicker that came from the R.A.'s halo.

The sight of it was enough to make Comstock's blood run cold. Hopelessly he wished for a heart attack that would make him *hors de combat,* but for once that organ seemed impregnable.

Then, crawling on his hands and knees, crawling after the unseen bulk of Bowdler, with fear in him like a live thing, Comstock died a thousand deaths. In the darkness a bulky body had bumped into him, and for a moment his heart had seemed to stop completely but then he realized it was only Grundy. The man had whispered, "Not far now."

Most frightening of all had been the moment when his head had touched the solid wall of the back room of the saloon. That had not been frightening in itself, but what had happened next was the worst of all, for suddenly the solid wall was no longer solid.

Frozen immobile, he had waited till Grundy had said, "Go on…hurry up."

Behind him Bowdler had pushed him, hard.

There was no choice. He went through the no longer solid wall.

Then there was another terrible period of darkness and silence and crawling along on all fours.

Bowdler finally spoke and he no longer whispered. He said, and his voice was harsh and loud, "It's all right now. We can stand up."

Then a light had flooded them.

And so here he was, Comstock thought dully, his brain feeling about as perceptive as a plate of liver as he stood in the small room that had no right to be where it was. Not that he knew where that was, but he knew that The Grandfather would certainly not approve of a hideout, and there could be no doubt that he was in such a place.

Grundy and Bowdler looked at him and enjoyed his manifest surprise.

Jimmy asked, "What, where, how, I mean…"

"We're not exactly fools, you know, Comstock old boy," Grundy said. "We knew that the R.A.'s had us under observation. We knew, too, that it was only a question of time before they came after us."

"But the saloon wall, how did we go through that?"

"Trap door, old sock, just a trap door." Bowdler grinned.

"And the tunnel we went through?" Comstock asked and then, looking around at the sybaritic furnishings of the little room, he asked, "This room, what is it?" Never in his life had he seen a room with such over-stuffed chairs, such soft warm colors, such a concern for creature comforts.

"Evidently," Bowdler said with an evil smirk, "Elmer Gantry 104 does not really believe in the Spartan virtues that he preaches so loudly."

"You mean this belongs to a Gantry?" Earlier, the very idea of being in a room that belonged to a Gantry would have made Comstock swoon, but his experiences were evidently toughening him, for aside from a certain feeling of breathlessness, and the knowledge that all the blood had left his face, and a sick feeling in the pit of his stomach, the blasphemous information did not affect Comstock at all.

Bowdler was standing with his back to Comstock, his hands linked behind his back, as he teetered back and forth from heels to toes and looked at some three-dimensional pictures that hung on Gantry's walls.

Only the fact that the n...e women in the round, true-color pictures were young, between twenty and thirty years old kept Comstock from a heart attack. If they had been older, the obscenity of their n....y would surely have made him pass out. He could not help wondering how Bowdler could seem to enjoy looking at the young women. It was incredibly revolting to Comstock's sense of the rightness of things.

"Sit down," Grundy said, "let's have a council of war."

Sitting on the very edge of the too-soft chair, keeping his back rigid, Comstock kept his attention glued on Grundy and Bowdler. Now perhaps, he would pick up some information of real value to the Fathers.

He noticed with some dismay that the other two men slouched back in their chairs and seemed to be enjoying the ease of their surroundings.

He asked uneasily, "Is there no chance that the R.A. will follow us here? Don't they know about this retreat?"

"Would any R.A. dare to contaminate a Gantry's home with his presence? Relax, Jimmy." Bowdler sprawled out, his large t...b hanging over one arm of the over-stuffed chair. "The only chance we're taking is that Gantry may come here. I checked and found that he is conferring with the Fathers' today."

How easily these two men spoke the terrible words. It made Comstock sit ever straighter on the very edge of the chair he occupied.

The cool air of the room, which seemed to have been washed and cleansed before entering the sacrosanct area was pleasant on Jimmy's heated face even while he wondered how a windowless room could be so aired.

"I gather," Bowdler said as he smiled at Jimmy's obvious consternation, "that you have never been in a home of one of the Thirty before?"

Dully, Jimmy shook his head no.

"You'll find, laddy boy, that this is a strange world we live in with many paradoxes that to Grundy and me, demand an explanation. It wasn't too long ago that we were like you and found only elderly ladies attractive. But you know, as soon as we found out that the Thirty like their women young, we too began to find something vastly exciting in youth."

SO ALARMED that he dare not continue to look at Bowdler, Jimmy looked around the room trying to find something to change the subject, some object on which to focus. On a book shelf nearby he saw one of his childhood favorites, and grabbed it with a feeling of relief.

It was a copy of Father Goose. He ran his eye over the first poem and drew from the verse of Jack and Jill the knowledge that the world had not gone insane. There, it was just as he remembered it,

"Jack and Jill went up the hill
To ….. a …. of water.
Jack fell down and broke his …..
And Jill came …….. after."

He riffled through the pages as Bowdler went on talking. On page ten was another favorite,

"Little Polly Flinders
Sat among the cinders
Warming her pretty little ….
Her mother came and caught her
And whipped her little daughter
For spoiling her nice new ……."

But the assurance of the known faded away as Bowdler's voice went rumbling on and on. "It occurred to both of us that perhaps there was some reason why we are brought up to esteem aged women so much. After all, if old ladies are as exciting as we are taught that they are, how come the Gantrys and others of the Thirty only have young concubines? This was one of the questions we asked ourselves, and we think we have the answer…"

Grundy broke in, "Have you ever wondered, Comstock, why it is that the only women who have children are the ones who are called up before the Fathers?"

This was even worse than the time Comstock's father had told him the "facts of life." Much worse, for what Grundy was intimating was at variance with what his father had taught him. It was worse.

"Maybe," Grundy said broodingly, "just maybe there is a damn good reason why the Fathers are called the Fathers!"

There are moments in life so terrifying that the very ground seems to shift beneath one's feet. That was the sensation that Comstock was experiencing. All was alien. He clung to the tattered copy of Father Goose as the only tangible thread that held his reeling sanity together. Averting his eyes from Grundy's and Bowdler's faces he hurriedly read,

"There was a little girl
Who had a little curl
Right in the middle of her ……..
And when she was good she was very, very good.
But when she was bad she was ……"

Even the familiar rhyme failed in its lulling purpose. He could no longer hide behind its chant-like curtain. Bowdler's voice went on, striking ever more harshly at the roots of Comstock's being.

"What a mockery all of our lives would be if what Grundy and I think is true. Suppose everything we have been taught is a lie. What then little man? What then?"

From some unknown and previously untapped reservoir of strength Comstock managed to dredge up the ability to say, "That's ridiculous. There would be no reason under the two suns for that to be true. The truth is mighty and will prevail."

"Just a little less of the copybook maxims if you don't mind, old man," Bowdler said. "Hear us out."

"Just suppose," Grundy bent his stocky middle body over so that he was closer to Comstock. "Just suppose for the sake of argument, that we are right. That our whole way of life is false. Look what that could mean."

Bowdler broke in, excitement making his voice harsh and rasping. "Suppose there is no real merit in old age. Suppose that the one-hundred-and-fifty year olds whose intelligence we worship as a matter of course, are really just senile old people! Then what?"

Grundy's face set. His mouth set in thin lines of derision. "I know for a fact, that the Elders, are just that. Elder. There's no magic in old age no matter what they taught us in school or what they keep yelling and yammering at us all the time. Old people are just old…"

Was there no end to the men's blasphemies? Comstock shook his aching head wearily. First they had attacked the peak of all things, The Grandfather. Next they had profaned the Fathers, and now the Elders. What sacred functionaries were left to attack? None, he realized with some relief. For the pyramid of his government was erected on the broad base of the Elders, who were guided and advised by the Fathers, who were in turn guided and led by that font of all knowledge, The Grandfather.

Taking a deep breath and setting his heavy jaw, Bowdler said, "If The Grandfather is a fake as I am beginning to believe, and the Fathers a pack of self-seeking sybarites who stay in power just because they are the most direct descendants from the original Thirty, and if the Elders are doddering fossils whose intellectual powers are supposed to befuddle us and keep us in place, than I say with Grundy, the time has come to overthrow this foul regime."

So there had been a final blasphemy left!

This one was so gigantic, the meaning Bowdler's words conveyed, so treasonable, that Comstock found himself waiting for the end. Just so far could men go and no further. These two must be wiped out, destroyed along with their poisonous statements.

The idea!

Overthrow The Grandfather? The very lightnings would, must come down and blast the two impious villains where they stood.

Comstock waited.

The lightnings, if they were coming, seemed long delayed.

But surely The Grandfather who was everywhere and knew all things must have overheard these infidels.

Why then did He not strike them down, limb and body?

It was only then, that in the very back of Comstock's mind a nervous little finger of doubt began to twist and turn, and finally asked a question.

"Suppose," the little finger scratched on the blackboard of his cortex, "suppose they're right...suppose The Grandfather is not all-powerful and all knowing?"

Then he waited for the lightnings to strike him too.

And all the while he wrestled with himself his two friends sat in strained silence, waiting...waiting...

No lightning.

Some of the tension began to drain out of Comstock, and as it did, Grundy and Bowdler exchanged knowing looks. Bowdler said at last. "Welcome."

"Welcome, Jimmy," Grundy smiled, "now you are one of us."

One of them.

He had exchanged the peace and security of resting in Grandfather's arms, of putting his weary head against Grandpop's long beard...Grandpop? How fast he was sliding... He had exchanged the surety of his life, for what?

For the friendship of two drinking companions. Somehow the swap did not seem to his advantage.

Bowdler seemed almost to be able to read his mind, for he said. "Buck up, Jimmy. You're going to find it's good to be a whole man. There are rewards!"

But all Comstock could remember was the ease and safety of that which he was surrendering. It came hard. Very hard.

"Growing up is always difficult," Bowdler said, his voice soft and full of understanding. "But I promise you there are rewards."

What rewards?

Before Comstock could put his question into words, there was a crashing sound at the door, the real door, not the hidden one by which they had entered the sacred precincts of the Gantry's room.

The primapara of the door trembled beneath the assault that was being launched on it.

Through the heavy wood they could hear the voice of authority. "Open up in the name of the R.A."

All a tremble, Comstock searched his friends' faces for reassurance.

He found none.

Bowdler said, "I don't understand it."

"No point in going back the way we came, the R.A. will have found that by now," Grundy said and his forehead was washboarded with worry.

CHAPTER FIVE

IF ONLY the R.A. had arrived a little earlier was all that Comstock was able to think. Five minutes earlier and his convictions would have been safe. He'd have been able to throw himself into the R.A.'s protection and tell all. That way would have meant safety and perhaps a reward.

But now?

Bowdler's bulky body moved toward the door. He yelled, "All right, keep your halo cool, I'm coming."

How, Comstock wondered, could anyone be so brave? No fear showed on Bowdler's granite-like face. None at all. His hand on the door knob, he paused and called back over his shoulder, "Grundy, come here, stand at this side of the door, you, Comstock, stand on the other side. I'll stall him, and if my plan works, you two beat it...fast! Grundy, you know where to take Comstock?"

"Sure, to Helen's," Grundy said and took up a position at the side of the door. Comstock, knees wobbling, hands sweating, stomach writhing, took up the position indicated for him.

Then Bowdler opened the door. He bowed derisively and said, his tones steady, the words ironical. "Won't you come in and make yourself comfortable?"

It was the same R.A. whose small features and lean hand had menaced them in the saloon.

His halo was bright with anger. His hand had the stun gun at the ready. The words that came from his mouth were bright with menace. He said, "I want you three to know that my gun is set to kill."

Now sweaty-footed fear was walking down Comstock's back. Never had he heard of an R.A. using the death control on his gun. Ordinarily just the threat of nervous stunning was enough to make the most irate submissive.

Long legs spread wide apart, hands on his hips, Bowdler said, "By what right do you enter the sanctum of a Gantry?"

"By the right invested in me by the Fathers and by my warrant from The Grandfather." The R.A.'s reedy voice was cold.

Throwing his big head back, Bowdler laughed in the man's face. He said, "Well, now, that sounds real important. But does it mean anything?"

Spread in a straight line, as the three men were, the R.A. could only menace one of them at a time. His gun went back and forth in a slow arc.

He said, "Put your hands behind your backs and come quiet-ly."

"Throw ourselves into the broad lap of The Grandfather, eh?" Bowdler asked and he seemed to be enjoying himself tremendously.

"Of course. He understands and He will judge your case according to its merits."

"And having understood our case, and having judged it in advance, He will have us 'removed' for the good of society?" Bowdler asked, but it was more of a statement than a question.

"That remains to be seen." the R.A. said.

"Humph," Bowdler grinned. "If we play it your way, our remains will be all that will be seen. No, thank you. I don't think I like that method at all."

With no warning and with no change of expression, Bowdler waited till the R.A.'s gun was pointed at Grundy at one end of its slow arc, then threw himself in a berserk charge straight at the R.A.

The R.A. hurriedly swung his gun back and pulled the trigger. He missed, and by that time Bowdler's long arms were around his knees and he was being dragged down to the soft carpet on the floor.

At the precise moment that the R.A. began to fall, Grundy gestured for Comstock to follow him and ran through the door. It took a second or so for Comstock's frozen muscles to obey his frightened brain, but then as the R.A. brought the gun up level with Bowdler's forehead and pulled the trigger, he ran.

The last sight he saw, as he chanced a look over his shoulder, was the sight of all intelligence draining out of Bowdler's face. The charge had hit him.

Slamming the door on the scene, Comstock ran, and as he ran he screamed to Grundy, "The R.A. killed him! He killed Bowdler."

Ten feet away the news made Grundy pause and almost stumble, but Comstock saw him recover and then run on. He yelled back to Comstock. "Tough. He was a good guy. But we gotta keep going or we'll be killed too."

The endless corridor through which they were running was dank and it was dark. There was no curve, no up or down. It was simply a black hole through which they ran and ran, and kept on running. When Comstock thought that he would never be able to breathe again, that his muscles could no longer bear his weight, that he must slump in a helpless heap and wait for death, he heard Grundy snap, "Ten feet more."

The words shot a new charge of adrenaline into Comstock. With a last surge of strength he darted after his friend's back. As a matter of fact he lunged full tilt into it because the darkness was so complete he could not see his hand before his face.

Grundy grunted, "Hold everything. I have to find the latch."

Another moment that seemed to stretch out far beyond the end of eternity and then, just as Comstock's strained ears heard footsteps running behind him in the dark, Grundy said, "There it is." And a door opened. Beyond was further darkness, but it was not as complete as the stygian blackness they were leaving. Falling through the doorway, Comstock fell to his face as Grundy slammed the door behind them.

"That'll hold the R.A. for a minute and that's all we need."

Lifting his head, forcing his trunk upwards from the ground, Comstock saw that they had come out on a street...he looked at it while his breath raced in and out of his tortured lungs...the street was familiar. It was the one that housed the b.....l to which he repaired once a month.

At the curb waiting, was an R.A.'s carriage. The team of astrobats waited patiently in harness, their too-pointed faces and four ears heavy with menace towards anyone who dared to approach them.

Staggering to his feet, Comstock felt Grundy's arm go around his shoulders. Grundy half carried, half pushed him into the carriage.

"But...we can't go in this..." Comstock gasped. "You know the penalty for even going near an R.A.'s carriage!"

A final push shoved Comstock onto the seat. Grabbing the wicked metal electro-whip, Grundy forced the recalcitrant astrobats into what those crotchety animals considered a gallop.

"The first person who sees us will call for help! We're not even dressed like R.A.'s..." Comstock said.

Grundy was kind. He said patiently, "Our halos will protect us."

LOOKING at Grundy's head, Comstock half expected to see the silvery sheen of the mark of an R.A. But there was no sign of one.

"Are you insane? We have no halos. Only the R.A. has them."

Whipping the team expertly, Grundy said, and his words were a sigh, "You have much to learn, Comstock. There are no halos except in the eye of the beholder."

"What does that mean?"

The carriage was racing by the b.....l now and Comstock was amazed to see the Madame, who was standing in the doorway, make the sign of reverence and obeisance as they raced by.

"The halos don't exist. They're just post-hypnotic suggestion implanted in our minds when we're kids. We're conditioned to see the halos when we see an R.A. We're in an R.A.'s carriage now and so anyone seeing us will see our halos. It's as simple as that. But then, you don't know what hypnotism is, do you?"

"No." Comstock said this humbly and at the moment he felt that he knew nothing at all. He turned and looked backwards.

Down the street behind them, the R.A., his halo shining brightly, like a good deed in an evil world, was pointing his gun at them. Comstock said, "The R.A. found the door. He's going to shoot us!"

Wordlessly, Grundy flicked the whip over the beasts' backs. The carriage swerved and carried them around the corner. Comstock could not tell if the R.A. had fired and missed, or had held his fire, for of course a stun gun is silent as the grave, and only affects the human nervous system.

Careening along the quiet streets Comstock found time to feel deep and real sorrow for Bowdler. It still did not seem possible that anyone could have been as brave as all that. Aloud he said, "Bowdler sacrificed himself for us, didn't he?"

Grundy nodded, his eyes alert, scanning the road ahead, for what? Comstock wondered.

"When you are doing what we are, you must be prepared for instant sacrifice," Grundy said.

"Hadn't we better give up?" Comstock asked. "Two of us against the entire world seems ridiculous. What chances have we?"

"None if you feel that way. But if you feel as Bowdler did and as I do, that it is worth anything to be a man, then it is worth while. Any chance is worth taking."

Grundy's tone changed. He said, "When I turn the next corner I'll slow the team down. When I do, jump out."

Jump out? What new madness was this? But before he had a chance to argue, Grundy had pulled hard on the bits and snapped, "Now!"

Rolling free of the carriage on his side, Comstock saw even as he fell to the ground, that Grundy had thrown himself out of the other side of the carriage.

The team raced on, dragging the empty carriage banging and clattering at their multiple heels.

Shaken, bruised, sore from head to foot, Comstock said as Grundy pulled himself to his feet. "Why did you do that?"

"Let the R.A.'s keep their radio tail on the carriage. A lot of good it'll do them!"

Grundy again helped him to his feet, and then said, "Follow me."

Comstock's mind was a whirl again. What was a radio?

The street was even quieter than most in Comstock's city. Small houses, a decent distance apart, lined the lawns where the purplish grass sparkled in the light of the twin moons.

The house that Grundy stopped in front of was identical with all the others. He took a key from his pocket and opened the door. Then he called out, "Helen!"

COMSTOCK had come a long way at that moment when he had waited futilely for The Grandfather's wrath to strike him dead, but he had not come to the point where he could watch the indecency of the scene that followed. Averting his eyes as the young girl entered the room, he wished desperately that he might be struck deaf so as not to have to hear what followed their entry.

In the first place she was obscenely young, not more than twenty-five. In the second place her ugly young skin was completely without wrinkles. In the third place she threw her round young arms around Grundy's neck, and in the fourth place she k.....d him hard and long on the l..s and in the fifth place she crooned to him l..e words that no one should ever be forced to hear.

"Darling, darling, darling," she said over and over again. "I've missed you so terribly, I've been so worried...but it's over and you're near me again."

"Dearest," Comstock could not help hearing Grundy say and his opinion of the man descended sharply, "My loveliest sweetheart."

Then their l..ps met again in a sustained and prolonged bit of pornographic action that left Comstock weak. Worse perhaps than the way they were pushing their l..s against each other was the way they had glued their bodies together.

He coughed trying to bring them back to their senses.

Grundy broke away from the girl. "Thank The Grandfather," Comstock thought, and then bit his lip as he realized that he no longer had the right to call on that name...

The girl said, "But where's Bowdler? Darling, what's happened...he hasn't been...he isn't hurt?"

"Worse, dear." And the man touched her hair. The sight made little horripilations go up and down the hair on the back of Comstock's head.

"He's not…dead?"

"Yes, my darling, but he died bravely trying to save us."

She bent her head reverently and Comstock was pleased to see that even so brazen a hussy was still not lost to all the common decencies.

Grundy cleared his throat and made an obvious effort to change the subject. He said, "I'm sorry, I've forgotten to have you meet our new friend." Grundy introduced them.

Horror piled on horror. Comstock's face whitened as the young girl walked to him, took his hand, shook it, and then impulsively k....d him on the cheek.

Thank Grandfather she stopped after an interminable moment and turned back to Grundy. She asked, her voice low and shaken, "But dearest, oh my dearest, what are we to do now? Bowdler was so strong, so sure of himself; he knew so much more than we do of what is really happening in this sick world of ours…what are we to do?"

There, it was happening again. Comstock averted his shocked eyes as Grundy put his hand on the girl's w....t and said, "You are to do nothing, my love. You'll stay here in safety. You know that Bowdler and I decided that this is a man's job, and it must stay that way. I'll take no chance of risking your lovely skin…"

Then he turned to Comstock and said decisively. "There's no use waiting any longer, taking chances, risking death the longer we wait. We'll eat, rest a bit, and then, we'll risk all!"

"You mean…" The girl let her voice fade away.

"Tonight, in half an hour," Grundy said, his face set and stern. "Comstock and I will go before the Board of Fathers and challenge The Grandfather!"

Some of his resolution faded and he said more quietly, "But how I wish Bowdler were with us. We three might have stood a better chance. But he had set the time as tonight, and I'll not be false to his trust."

Half an hour, Comstock thought dully. It wasn't long to live...not long enough at all...

CHAPTER SIX

IN ONE way the half-hour just vanished. In another, it lasted longer than all the rest of Comstock's life put together. While he stood in the doorway, his back to Grundy and the impassioned l..e scene that Helen and Grundy were enacting as what might be their last farewell, he wondered how thirty minutes, which had seemed to go on so long, seemed to fly past so quickly.

He could hear Grundy almost moan, "'Helen thy beauty is to me as...'" and then harsh and strident, drowning out all other sound, seeming like the sound that was the ultimate that human ears could ever bear to hear there came an enormously amplified voice.

Comstock had never heard The Grandfather speak, and yet, now hunching himself into a pre-natal ball, his hands pressed tight against his ears, he knew that no other voice could have held that command, that awe-inspiring tone, that this voice held which now threatened to deafen him permanently.

The words that smote at Comstock were, "I am displeased."

Grundy ran to Comstock, gripped him by the shoulders, pulled Comstock's hands away from his ears and roared, "Follow me! They've got a speaker hidden someplace near here. I never knew they'd found Helen."

The girl's face was washed clean of every emotion but that of anger. She stood at Grundy's side, her hands on her hips and the words she spat out, hurt Comstock's ears even more than the larger than life roar of The Grandfather.

She said, "What a cheap trick!"

"Darling, I can't leave you here now. You must come with us," Grundy's face was tortured.

"I know," she assented and waited for his orders.

Somehow Comstock forced himself to his feet. He would not, could not, allow himself to be shamed by this girl child. It was unmanly.

The voice of The Grandfather said, "My grandchildren are being naughty. I do not like this conduct. I am afraid, very afraid that you three need punishment."

The tones mumbled a long time after the words were no longer separable. It was like the aftermath of thunder. Comstock moaned in horrified torment.

All his fears were back. The Grandfather was omnipotent just as he had always been taught. And yet, and yet…that little canker of doubt in the back of his head kept muttering, if that were so, how could the girl have called it all a cheap trick? Were there even more things, that he, Comstock, did not understand?

As far as his fevered eye could see there was no sign of humanity. Comstock knew that behind the drawn blinds of the houses on the street people like him were huddled in fear, hoping desperately that the voice did not refer to them.

Grundy said, "If they've got a speaker planted near here, that means we're under surveillance."

"Of course," Helen agreed, "that's obvious. What do we do about it?"

"I wish I'd never gotten you involved in this, dear," Grundy said.

"I'm glad. For if you hadn't, we'd never have had what little we have had out of life. I think it's been worth it, and more."

The smile on Grundy's face was so radiant, the renewed courage he clearly had received from what she said, made Comstock think that perhaps Bowdler had been right, perhaps there were indeed rewards for being a whole man.

Grundy blew a kiss to Helen, and then a smile that oddly enough reminded Comstock of Bowdler crossed his face. He walked from the entrance of the house out into the center of the street. Then, feet separated, again so like Bowdler, his hands on his hips, he threw his head back and looking at the sky he roared out a challenge.

"Come and get us! Don't treat us like sorry grandchildren, come and get us. I dare you!"

Across the street Comstock saw a curtain being pulled slightly to one side. Then a frightened eye stared out. The Grandfather or his representatives would have to answer Grundy's challenge he realized with a little thrill of pride.

The powers-that-be dared not allow the people to see a man defy The Grandfather.

It was, Comstock thought, rather a wonderful thing to be a rebel.

But the feeling passed quickly when, with a speed that defied his understanding, a kind of vehicle he had never before seen appeared roaring out of the distance. It had four wheels, and a carriage-like body, but no team of astrobats drew it. Instead it seemed to be propelled by magic. It was rather a noisy magic for a series of explosions seemed to come from the front of it constantly.

Above the low roar of the carriage's explosions rose the voice of The Grandfather. "I have dispatched a chariot for you. Beware my wrath and come quietly."

Helen looked jubilant. She said, "We're forcing their hand. This is the first time in centuries they've found it necessary to use a car!"

"If we only had more strength," Grundy said, "I'd almost be optimistic. We sure have them worried."

Then the object Helen had called a "car" drew up in front of them and a door opened. Four of the leanest, hardest R.A.'s that Comstock had ever seen pointed stun guns at the three of them. The man, who sat behind a wheel said, "Get 'em in quick. No sense in having too many of these slobs see this car."

Comstock flashed a look of inquiry at Grundy.

"Sure let's join them. It's easier to be driven there, than to have to walk as I'd figured."

The vehicle was obviously not designed to hold seven people and since the four R.A.'s drew away from Helen with the same kind of sick disquietude that Comstock had felt, the small remaining space left for Grundy, the girl and Comstock made them all wedge in rather tightly.

Helen's flesh was soft and warm, Comstock realized with a shock, and the clean, sweet smell of her in his flaring nostrils was a warning that Bowdler and Grundy might well be right. There was something about young women...something unlike the emotion he had felt on his monthly visits to his elderly lady friends in the b+.....l.

The "car" raced through the deserted streets with a speed that would have scared Comstock out of a year's growth if he had not had so many other larger worries tearing at him.

MOST baffling to him was the fact that despite the fact that they were going before a tribunal, which would sentence them to death, Grundy was able to lean closer to Helen and whisper to her a poem that Comstock had never heard before and the words of which failed to make any sense.

He was saying, "Is this the face that launched a thousand ships?"

And then he k+....d her.

In the Grandfather's "car" with four R.A.'s right there, Grundy was k+.....g Helen!

It was flabbergasting to Comstock and in a strange way that he could not quite understand he felt a little pang of jealousy. He found he would have liked to have had a Helen next to him... Someone young and brave...and soft...and warm...who smelled like the girl now pressed so close against him.

Something of what he was thinking must have communicated itself to the girl for she turned from her beloved and said, "Poor Comstock. It's not as though you were all alone. We're with you."

Then her full-soft lips were pressed on his forehead.

The blood pounding into his head made his face flare crimson.

Sounds of disgust from the four R.A.'s made him angry instead of upset as they might have.

What did they, poor fools, know of the feelings of a rebel? Of a...hero?

The kiss buoyed him up all the way to the House of the Fathers. But then, when the ominous, tall, round building rose up in front of them, and he could see the two circular perispheres at the base of the trylon-like structure, fear returned.

In one of the completely round low buildings was the House of the Fathers. The other, on the right hand side, was the meeting place of the Elders. And high above in the very tip of the tall round building was The Grandfather's Retreat.

It was awe-inspiring because never before had he been closer to it than a mile and that only on those days sacred to the memory of The Grandfather.

The car jolted to a halt right in front of the trylon.

The R.A.'s hustled the three of them out of the vehicle. Where were they to be taken? Comstock watched wide-eyed. Their guards took them past the door on the right. So they were not to be taken before the Elders...

There was no sign that they were going to be forced over to the left. That meant they were not to go before the Fathers.

Instead they were marched through the center door.

Breathing became almost impossible for Comstock. They were being taken into The Grandfather's Retreat.

Never before had he heard of such a thing happening. But then, of course, never before had anyone challenged The Grandfather. At least not to Comstock's knowledge.

Inside the doorway there were broad windows. Through one of them Comstock could see into the room where all the Elders were met in solemn conclave. Their aged incredibly wise faces were heavy with responsibility. All of the seamed faces were turned so that the Elders could see the three who had defied authority.

The force of all the red-rimmed eyes staring at Comstock was enough to turn his knees to jelly. Instantly Grundy was at his side, words of encouragement on his lips.

He said, "Forget the old codgers. They're so senile they don't even know what's happening."

In some way Grundy's blasphemy was like a jolt of fresh air, or a couple of corpse revivers. With the thought of liquor, Comstock suddenly realized that he should be sick. His head should be bothering him. It had been ages and ages since he had had a drink. And yet, despite all the alarums and excursions, his heart had not bothered him. That was odd…

But all thought, and almost all consciousness ebbed away when that voice came thundering down.

It said, "Take them before The Fathers before you bring them to me!"

The R.A.'s paused in their tracks and then changed the direction in which they had been going.

Ahead was the biggest door that Comstock had ever seen. Discreetly lettered on it was a sign. It read, "The Fathers."

The leader of the R.A.'s opened the door and then Helen, Grundy and he were pushed through the door into an anteroom. It was small and on the far side of it was an even bigger door than the one by which they had entered.

All around the walls of the little room were chairs.

Comstock realized with horror that the door was all that separated them from the united might of the Fathers. They must be meeting in solemn conclave, deciding what should be done with the three guilty ones.

And then the R.A.'s left, their halos shining more brightly than Comstock had ever seen any R.A.'s halo shine.

The three were alone.

The Fathers in the next room, and above all brooding in titanic majesty was The Grandfather…waiting…

Helen sat down, crossed her legs, with a flourish that revealed not only her slim a+….s but, Comstock gulped as he watched in awed fascination, he could see her c+....s! They were round and full.

Throwing himself into a chair next to her, Grundy said, "It's their next move, blast them. I hope they hurry it up."

Unable to do anything but pace back and forth, sneaking an occasional look at Helen's l+..s, Comstock brooded about what had happened to him.

Nightmarish in essence, he yet wondered whether it hadn't been worth it. He was no braver than ever, but there were new emotions, new sensations raging through him. After all, he was a man. And as a man, he was, when all was said and done, capable of being a father. For that matter right at that moment, and looking almost boldly at Helen's c+....s, he felt that he would kind of like to be a real Father. Not with Helen, after all she was Grundy's, but with some other girl like her...

He had not ever felt that way about any of the elderly ladies he had seen, and certainly never with the woman he visited once a month.

Turning he faced the door behind which the Fathers were sitting and considering his case. The arrogance of them! To think that if his friend's hypothesis was correct, these men had their pick of all the young girls on the planet with whom to... Even then, he could not think the word, but the anger was real.

He still could not watch when Grundy k+....d Helen and touched her, but he found that it was for a different reason.

Then Helen gasped and Grundy swore, and Comstock turned to look in the direction of their gaze.

The door of the Fathers' room had opened.

And through it walked Bowdler. Big as life!

CHAPTER SEVEN

BOWDLER'S smile was as warm as ever, and his face was just as alive as it had been before Comstock saw it glaze in death. He said, "Take it easy, kids. I'm alive. Really I am."

Then all three, Grundy, Helen, and Comstock spoke at once, their words garbled, their tones excited. Bowdler held up one meaty hand and said, "Hold everything. The R.A. lied when he said that his stun gun was set to kill. That's all there is to it. I came to shortly after you both got away."

Grundy and Helen were at Bowdler's side, Grundy pump--handling his friend's hand, Helen hugging him with relief. But Comstock stood off to one side and considered this miraculous return from death. Why, he wondered almost coldly, had the R.A. lied? What function would it serve? Had it served?

Bowdler must have felt Comstock's thoughts for he turned and said, "There was a reason, Comstock. Truly there was, and a good one."

The seriousness in Bowdler's tone made Helen and Grundy draw back a little. Then they retreated in sudden panic at his next words, for Bowdler said, "You see, my friends, I ordered the R.A. to lie to you."

Perhaps because Grundy had been a friend of Bowdler's longer or perhaps because Comstock had been pushed as far as a man can be pushed, for whatever reason, or combination of reasons, Comstock suddenly found himself for the first time in all his wild adventure taking the initiative. He snapped, "No one can give an R.A. an order but a Father!"

Bowdler smiled, "That's right, Comstock. Good work, boy. You *have* come a long way."

It was Grundy who gasped, "Then you are a Father?"

Nodding, Bowdler said, "Yes."

Before they could question Bowdler any further, he suddenly put his finger to his lips in the immemorial gesture for silence. Then he pointed at the closed door behind which the Board of Fathers were sitting in solemn conclave. Bowdler whispered, "We've only got a split second before you are called up before them."

"What can we say, what can we do?" Grundy pleaded.

"I thought," Bowdler said, his brow furrowed with worry, "that I'd be in a position to fight for you all by this time. But

141

my plan didn't work out. They're furious at your effrontery. I'm afraid if you go before them now they'll sentence you to death."

Comstock looked around him wildly. Life had become much more sweet to him in the last few days and he didn't intend to give it up without a battle.

Bowdler said, "If I could only spirit you all away to safety…"

That was when the door opened. A uniformed emissary of the Fathers, his regalia frightening in its black severity, came through the doorway. He was to the left of Comstock.

He barked, "Follow me." Then, sure in the arrogance of power, he turned his back on Comstock and the others and began to walk back towards the door. It was obvious that the thought that they might not follow him had not even crossed his mind.

Grundy made a signaling motion to Comstock, a chopping gesture with the side of his hand that puzzled Comstock mightily. Seeing that Comstock was baffled, Grundy brought the edge of his hand down in the same chopping motion on Helen's neck. Then he pointed at the black garbed man who was leading the way into…death…

Once the idea penetrated Comstock's considerably bemuddled mind he sprang into action as though he had been trained in violence all his life. Leaping closer to the emissary he whacked the edge of his hand down on the nape of the man's neck.

As he did so, Grundy and Bowdler ran to join him. They caught the man before he hit the ground. Comstock stood stock still, and looked at his hand in some wonder. The idea! His hand had struck down a member of the inner circle of the Fathers' Right Arms! Incredible!

As though the whole thing had long ago been rehearsed in its entirety, Helen pushed the door closed, hiding completely what had just happened.

All the while that Comstock stood and gloried in his own daring, the others were busy ripping the uniform from the unconscious man's body.

Bowdler was grunting from the effort, his big beefy face almost vermilion with strain. He had yanked off the guard's trousers and was now holding them up in front of Grundy, as if estimating how they would fit.

"Nope." He grunted, and then threw the pants to Comstock. "They'd never fit Grundy. You'll have to wear the uniform."

Still bemused, for otherwise the wry thought of doing what he was, would have made him faint, Comstock stripped off his own trousers—in front of Helen!—and put on the guard's. While he was busy dressing Bowdler said, "The only thing I can see to do is for you to try to escape from here, with Comstock masquerading as an R.A. Meanwhile, I'll join the Fathers and see if I can distract them long enough to let you three get away."

"But where will we go?" Helen asked. "They've found out about me, and my house."

"I know, I know," Bowdler grunted impatiently. "Let me think."

By that time Grundy had helped Comstock into the form fitting black jacket. The final touch was the menacing slouch hat that went with the uniform.

Comstock drew himself up proudly. This was living! Of course, he thought, and the idea made him deflate his chest rapidly; if they were caught now, their deaths would be even more unpleasant... But he patted the evil little stun gun at his hip, and tried to feel very, very brave.

The man on the floor, looking highly undignified in his long underwear, and not at all menacing, stirred uneasily, and moaned. Bowdler bent down and rapped him on the point of his chin, and the man relaxed into deep unconsciousness again.

Not willing to be put off any longer, Comstock asked, "Bowdler, since you're a Father, why are you doing what you're doing?"

"No time for that, boy, no time at all."

Grundy added his curiosity, "But we must know, Bowdler, we can't keep up this insane hare and hounds chase unless we know what's going on!"

Bowdler pushed Grundy and Helen towards Comstock and snapped, "Later, later. For now, all I can say is that I am fed up with the unfairness of the way our world is being run. I went out into your world to try and find rebels to use as the nucleus for a revolution. But there's no time now for any further explanations. Listen to me carefully. The guards at the front entrance would recognize you, Comstock, even in that uniform, so you must escape by the back exit. To get to it, turn right when you leave here, go to the end of the long hall, and then turn left, follow that passage to its end and then turn right. That'll lead you to the garage. Commandeer a car and go to 14 Anthony Comstock Road. I'll join you as soon as I safely can."

"Right, left, right." Grundy said. "Okay, Bowdler. I hope you can join us soon."

"Before you go," Bowdler said, "sock me on the jaw."

Grundy asked, "Hit you? Why should I?"

"Do as he says," Helen said impatiently. "He has to have an alibi for our escape."

Closing his eyes, Grundy lashed out suddenly. His fist missed Bowdler's chin and landed high on his cheek near Bowdler's eye. He snorted in annoyance, but said, "All right, all right, that'll have to do. Now run!"

Throwing himself on the thickly carpeted floor he imitated the truly unconscious man who was slumped there.

Lifting his head he said, "Beat it! Go on...hurry!"

They left.

COMSTOCK chanted to himself over and over again as they walked down the long impressive marble corridor, right, left, right. What was behind the doors they passed? Would he ever know? Each one seemed more menacing than the one before it.

And somehow, high above him, Comstock could feel the brooding majesty of The Grandfather. Surely here in the buildings that were sacred to Him, The Grandfather must know what they were doing. His knees shook and his stomach turned over as he thought of the effrontery of what they were doing.

If one of the doors that lined the corridor had so much as squeaked, Comstock thought, he would die. He knew it. He knew his weak heart would not be able to stand the strain and that was all there was to it.

The silence that surrounded them was harrowing.

Grundy, his arm around Helen protectively, kept his eyes busy searching, hoping against hope that no one would see them, question them...or suspect them.

Comstock's palm and fingers were sweaty with the agony of the grip he had on the butt of the stun gun.

Ahead of them was the end of the corridor and no one had seen them.

Taking an even deeper breath, Comstock strode to the left. The other two followed in his footsteps. This corridor was shorter, he was grateful to see, and the one that went off to the right at the end of it seemed lighter. At least it did not seem quite as dark and gloomy as the way they had come.

And then they had come to the end of the last hallway and ahead was the door that Bowdler said led to escape. But the highest hurdle, Comstock thought, was still ahead. They had to steal an auto from a garage. He had learned that the astrobatless-carriage that had conveyed them there was called an auto, but what in the world was a garage?

He hoped it wasn't some new horror.

All three of them froze. The door that led outdoors was opening.

Grundy had to nudge Comstock in the ribs to make him move. For the sight of a platoon of black-garbed R.A.'s stretching off into the middle distance that was revealed when the door opened had been enough to end any and all thoughts of resistance on the part of Comstock.

The leader of the R.A.'s snapped a salute at Comstock, which he answered only when Grundy's elbow dug deeply into his rib cage. The R.A. Leader said, "Reporting to The Fathers!"

Comstock made a gesture that he hoped would look as if he was giving the Leader permission. It was obvious from the way the man was behaving that he thought Comstock outranked him. And as Comstock, Grundy and the girl passed the platoon, it occurred, to Comstock that any R.A. who was employed at this fountainhead would of necessity outrank any others.

The platoon stood at frozen-faced, stiff-backed attention as the trio left the back door and walked across the greensward toward a building that Grundy whispered to Comstock must be the garage.

When they were out of earshot of the platoon, Comstock sneaked a look back over his shoulder. The black-garbed men, like automatons, were marching into the building.

Grundy said, "Okay, so we've found the garage, but how are we going to drive the car? That's the next big question."

Comstock was too relieved, first by the fact that they had escaped the R.A.'s and second by the fact that the garage had turned out to be just a building, to take on any new worry for a while.

Smiling a little, Helen said, "Hold on, Bowdler said we were to take a car, therefore, it must be easy to drive one; or else we'll have to force an R.A. to drive it for us."

"I suppose you're right," Grundy said, but he sounded dubious.

"If we make an R.A. drive it for us, that'll mean we're stuck with him," Comstock said. "I don't think we want one of them around, do we?" Then he saw a black uniform and he snapped, "Quiet!"

The man saluted as, Grundy in the lead, Helen following him, and Comstock bringing up the rear, they entered the "garage". Comstock said, "I have been ordered by the Fathers to take these prisoners on a journey."

The black uniform was dirty and greasy which surprised Comstock. He'd never before seen an R.A. who was not spotless. However, when he saw what the man had been working on he was no longer surprised. The man waved a filthy hand at an object on four wheels and said, "Try this one. I'm having a lot of trouble with these blasted things." He shook his head. "If we only had some new parts. I don't know how much longer I can keep stealing parts from one car and putting them in another."

Comstock had to make a decision. His hand still on his stun gun, he said to Grundy, "Get behind that wheel, and let's get started."

Slightly taken aback, Grundy gulped and then said, "Yes sir. Right away, sir."

There was no other way that Comstock could see that it could be done. An R.A. would not have driven the car and allowed the two prisoners to sit idly in the back of the conveyance.

The dirty uniformed man, mumbling under his breath, got down on all fours and began to tinker with the underneath part of the "car" he had been working on when they entered the "garage".

That was a bit of luck for it allowed Grundy to enter the "car," get behind the wheel and examine the various controls. Comstock and Helen sat grandly in the back seat and waited.

Finally, after a long wait, Comstock leaned forward and whispered to Grundy, "Better get started before he gets suspicious."

He was a little shocked at the curses that Grundy directed at him. They ended by the man saying, "All right, genius, you tell me what to do."

The dirty man's legs were all that showed from the place where he was working. Comstock leaned over Grundy's shoulders and said, "What about that key? It seems to be part of the works."

Shrugging, Grundy turned the key. There were a lot of things sticking up out of the floor and Comstock said, "They look like feet would fit on them, don't they?"

Sticking out one foot experimentally, Grundy said, "Hmm...yes, they do."

Then there was a series of explosions, and a sudden jolting start that threw Comstock into Helen's lap.

LATER, when they had learned a bit about driving, they were all very grateful that the "car" had been pointed at the opening in the door when it started, for they knew that they would never have been able to figure out how to reverse it.

Their vehicle bucked and bounced as it roared out through the doorway. It was only after the first thirty seconds of movement that Grundy remembered that the other driver had held his hands on the wheel.

Trying this, he found that the car responded to his touch. Rather delighted, he turned the wheel sharply. Instantly Comstock was thrown off Helen's lap onto the floor of the "car". She landed on top of him driving the breath out of his lungs in a gasp that he momentarily feared was so noisy that The Grandfather, perched high in his tower, would hear.

But the sound of the explosions in the front of the car drowned out all other noises.

Careening down the esplanade away from the frightening buildings, away from the Fathers and The Grandfather, Comstock finally managed to push Helen off of him and get back into the seat. She was grinning excitedly and he found that he too shared in the feeling. In the front seat Grundy called back, "Hey, this is kind of fun!"

It stopped being fun when it became necessary to turn a corner. This was a difficult maneuver and when it was over, Helen and Comstock were again entwined in a manner that was highly indecent. Now that the buildings they had escaped from were receding into the distance, Comstock found that he was rather enjoying the feel of Helen's soft flesh.

It made him blush and his heart must have suffered from the strain, but nevertheless he did, he told himself, enjoy being near her. What a ghastly perversion! To find youth exciting! What would his dear Father have thought?

But then he decided not to worry too much about Father. One thought was uppermost in his mind. He wanted a girl just like Helen. If one could be found.

Grundy yelled above the sound the vehicle was making. "We're almost there. What number house did Bowdler say?"

"Fourteen, I think," Comstock said and he was glad to have a break in the direction that his thoughts were taking.

Next to him, Helen pursed her full lips and whistled. She said, "Take a look…"

The house well repaid a look. It was the closest that Comstock had ever been to a home that belonged to one of the Fathers. Immense, sprawling, with a lawn that was as carefully tended as time and work could make it, crisp bushes, trimmed and shaped, the house was a gem. It was on the side of a hill that sloped steeply downwards.

They drew up in front of it and a new problem arose. Grundy yelled, "Better jump. I don't know how to stop this thing!"

One after the other they leaped from the "car" which, since Grundy did not know how to shift the gears was still in first and was making all of fifteen miles an hour.

Rolling over and over, hands and knees badly scraped, Comstock thought, "There must be a better way than that to get out of a "car." But then, as the vehicle sped faster and faster down the decline of the hill, he said, "Grundy…Helen… Did you notice anything odd on the way here?"

They were picking themselves up and Grundy was being, Comstock thought, a little too solicitous about Helen and whether she was hurt, so he repeated himself a little more loudly.

"Odd?" Grundy finally said after he had patted Helen in various places, in none of which it seemed to Comstock, it had been likely for the girl to have injured herself. "What do you mean?"

"Don't you realize we didn't pass a single human being all the way here?"

"You're right," Helen said. "That is peculiar…"

Grundy looked about them. There was no one in sight. No one at all. That was not too peculiar, not here, not this near a Father's house, but the other streets should have been full of people… It was all very strange.

Down at the bottom of the hill the driverless "car" crashed into a tree. It was the only sound but for their breathing. Helen shivered.

Comstock said, "Let's get in the house. Quickly."

It was one thing, Comstock thought, to have been in a room that belonged to a Gantry, as they had been, but it was a completely different and much more frightening thing to be walking up the path to a house that belonged to a Father, even one like this that belonged to Bowdler who certainly had seemed to be friendly.

They were on the steps of a broad pleasant verandah now, and the entrance to the house was directly in front of them. The door was white, and had neatly lettered on it, "Enter."

Comstock grabbed Helen's free hand, her other was in the fold of Grundy's arm. Then all of them moved slowly towards the door.

It opened before Comstock could put his hand on the knob.

It swung wide enough for them to see that no one had opened it for them.

From inside the house, a heavy metallic voice said, "Welcome may you be."

CHAPTER EIGHT

PERHAPS the single, most frightening thing in the big living room to Comstock was the fact that the walls were solid with books. The cases ran from the floor to the ceiling and every available space was stuffed helter skelter with books, books and more books. In all his life it is highly unlikely that Comstock had ever seen more than ten or fifteen books at one time, and then only in what passed for a library in his culture.

Why, he thought, there must be thousands of books here. On what subjects could the authors have written? What was there to write that much about? A small hope persisted for a moment that maybe, for some strange reason most of the books might be duplicates. But that was eradicated when he looked at the odd, mysterious titles of the volumes. There were no duplicates and seemingly the books were divided up into categories. But some of the categories were so strange to Comstock that they passed his ability to comprehend.

What, he wondered, could sociology be? Or anthropology, or psychology, or these massive volumes full of poems...not simple enjoyable poems like Father Goose, but queer, abstruse ones, whose words made no sense at all to Comstock's reeling brain.

While he hurried around the room blowing dust off the tops of the books he was looking at, Helen and Grundy were concerned with who had greeted them on their entrance.

Leaving Comstock to his perusal of the shelves, Grundy tiptoed out of the room, and then looking in no particular direction, he called, "Hello? Who are you! Where are you?"

The same metallic voice answered, "I am the house. I am here to supply your wants, to feed you and make you comfortable."

When Comstock heard this the shock was too much for him. He swayed, and then sank, with an armful of books, into the deep recesses of an easy chair. A cloud of dust surrounded him. Instantly a whirring sound emanated from a screened section of the floor and he felt rather than saw the dust disappearing.

Considerably shaken, Grundy came back into the library. Helen said. "What do you suppose it is, darling?"

"Bowdler has told me about robots...machines that act almost like we do, but I never, ever, thought that one could run a whole house this way!"

Comstock was willing to accept the robot as he would have the word fairy when he was a child and he was even more inclined to confuse the two things, when at Grundy's mention of being hungry, the door swung open and a wheeled cart entered loaded down with food the like of which none of the three had ever seen.

Sitting in a rather numb silence the three people stared at the food. But then the odors that came from it were too much for them and disregarding the magic of its appearance they ate as they never had before.

That was the beginning, for Grundy and Helen and Comstock of an enchanted month. At first, from minute to minute, they expected pursuit, and capture. But as time passed happily by, as every fleeting fancy was instantly taken care of by the house, they relaxed, and what was most important, began to devote almost all their waking hours to the books that confronted them on every side, in every room of the house.

No one ever seemed to pass the house, they heard no sounds from outside. They were in a charmed circle, in which every desire was instantly fulfilled.

Comstock was not aware of how and when it happened, but soon he was not even embarrassed at the sight of Grundy and Helen kissing and caressing each other. He no longer wanted to swoon when he heard them exchange love words. But what did happen was that he wanted some one like Helen more and more as time went on.

At first they waited impatiently for Bowdler to put in an appearance, but when days passed and there was no sign of him they ceased to expect him. Then worry began to take the place of expectancy. Suppose, they'd say, suppose he was found out by the Board of Fathers...was a Father ever punished? They did not know.

Occasionally, but only very occasionally, Comstock would put his hand to his chest and wonder why his heart disease no longer troubled him, but a question which is unanswerable ceases in some cases to be a question, and he almost forgot about it most of the time.

Then too, the contents of the books, which they were devouring with such avidity, were so exciting that it almost seemed that there was not enough time in one day for all the reading they wanted to do.

They'd rise in the morning and the instant they sat up in their respective beds, the doors of their bedrooms would open, wheeled carts would enter their room, and the house would serve them their breakfasts.

Having risen, clean clothes would be supplied. Then they'd hurry to the library, discuss what they'd been reading and then, undisturbed except by luncheon and dinner, they'd read, read, read.

SOMETIMES the house would seem to feel that they were devoting too much time to books and it would suddenly and magically produce games and they'd play away an evening.

But when the morrow dawned the lure of the books would call them back.

Their biggest problem was in deciding which of the books they read were fact and what fiction. This was their only noteworthy argument. One morning for instance, Comstock said, "I found a wonderful old book last night filled with reports on criminals. Fascinating! One of them was about a court in some kingdom or other back on earth where a prince found out that his stepfather had murdered his real father in order to marry his mother."

"I remember that one," Helen said. "It ended with practically everyone in the court murdered."

"That's the one," Comstock nodded.

"Y' know," Grundy said, "I wonder if that was really a report on actual criminals."

"Must have been," Comstock argued, "no fiction writer would have had the prince dilly dally the way that one did, never able to make up his mind what to do. Only in real life do people bumble along that way."

"Mmm…" Grundy disagreed. "I think a fine writer might have done just that in order to make the character seem real."

"Prince Hamlet *must* have been real," Comstock said. "He could not have been imagined. No, I'm sure that is fact. But this book I'm reading now, what nonsense!"

He held up Gibbon's "Decline and Fall of the Roman Empire."

"What an imagination! Fantastic!" Shaking his head he went on with his reading.

It was a day or two later when he was reading what he considered another criminal report, the story of a Moor and jealousy that the idea occurred to him.

Putting down the book, he stared thoughtfully off into space. The idea had just never entered his brain before. Was it possible, he wondered, that he might be able to woo Helen away from Grundy?

Not knowing a thing about how to go about it interfered quite a bit, he found. His flirtation, if you could call it that, began to resemble a game of hide and go seek, for he would lurk in dark corners of the house and wait for Helen to walk by alone.

Then, darting out, he'd try to manufacture love talk, or what seemed to pass for it in the book he'd been reading. One day, having succeeded in scaring Helen half out of her wits, by popping out of a linen closet and appearing at her side completely unexpectedly, he made a groping motion and managed to capture one of her hands. Bending over it, he kissed it.

That surprised Helen almost as much as his darting out of the closet and she was even more surprised when he said, his voice low, so that Grundy in the next room would not hear him,

"Helen…I…" But then his voice vanished and he was unable to go on with the speech he had prepared.

One eyebrow raised so high that it almost succeeded in touching her hairline, Helen considered him. Then she asked, "Is anything wrong? Do you feel all right?" Then she put her hand on his forehead and said, "Are you feverish?"

The speech that should have come tumbling out of his mouth raced through his mind, he thought, "Yes, I am feverish, burning with desire… Nothing can put out the fire but you…" That is what he thought. What he said, was, "Umm…I guess I am feeling sick. I think I'll go up and lay down for a while." Then tottering off he left her there.

Lying down, even with a cool cloth on his head, he found did not suffice to quench the fire that was threatening to consume him.

Returning to his reading he found that on occasion, Earthmen had murdered the men who stood in the way of their desire. Then it was that he began to trail Grundy instead of Helen. He'd stand in a doorway, while Grundy innocently read, and think of ways to kill his friend. Poison, he found in his reading, was one of the commoner ways of removing the other lover. That would have been fine and he'd have been glad to poison Grundy but for the small fact that he didn't have the vaguest idea what poison was.

And, what if he killed Grundy and even then Helen didn't fall in love with him? That was a big factor and one that succeeded in baffling him for quite a while. Perhaps, he decided finally, he'd better make sure she at least liked him before he went to the slightly extreme extent of murdering his friend.

But before he could take matters of any kind in hand, there came an interruption in the even tenor of their ways. Precisely a month after they entered Bowdler's house, the door opened and Bowdler came through the entrance, a broad smile of inquiry on his heavy face.

He asked no questions about how they were making out, he told them nothing about what he had been doing. Instead he asked, "Has she arrived yet?"

"She?" The word was chorused by the trio.

"Yes," Bowdler said, his expression changing and worry showing on it. "She should have been here by now if she escaped from the R.A.'s." Shaking his head, he sat down in one of the big comfortable chairs that were scattered all around the library. "She's the best possibility I've found since you three. Courageous, with a real brain in her head. I hope she's not been captured."

GRUNDY, Comstock and Helen stifled the questions, which were crowding to their lips, questions about the house, about the books, about the reason for their having been sequestered so long. In the face of Bowdler's worry, their questions seemed picayune.

"When should she have arrived?" Comstock asked.

"This morning. I helped her get away last night, gave her directions, and then turned off the force field that's been protecting the house and you three in my absence. If she doesn't appear soon, I'll have to turn it back on. I can't risk having the R.A.'s stumble on this retreat of mine."

"Force field?" Grundy asked timorously.

"Sure, a smaller version of the thing that the last scientists built to protect our whole planet from interlopers. Unseen, it blankets the whole area around the house in an invisible sheath that keeps anyone from even being aware of the house."

So that, Comstock thought, was why they had heard no one, seen no one passing by.

Bowdler got up from his chair and began to pace the floor uneasily. "It's getting later. I'd better turn the force field back on, even though it means that she'll never get here. Sometimes sacrifice is essential."

Rather to Comstock's surprise, he got to his feet, jutted out his rather insignificant jaw and said, "I'm going looking for her!"

"Good boy!" Grundy said approvingly.

Helen asked, "But how will you manage to get back even if you find her?"

"I don't know. All I know is that I can't rest thinking of someone wandering around at the mercy of the Father's Right Arms."

"I've got it," Bowdler said, slowly. "You go ahead, Comstock. Look for her to the east, down around Puritan Square. That's the direction from which she would be coming, if she's not been captured. Then, at twelve midnight, and twelve noon, I'll turn off the field for exactly thirty seconds each day and night till you return." The *if* was unspoken

"Shall I go dressed in the R.A.'s uniform or as a citizen?" asked Comstock.

"Umm..." Bowdler pulled at his lip thoughtfully, then said, "I'd go as a private individual. That way there should be fewer problems."

Helen asked the question that should have occurred to Comstock. "How will he know her?"

"She's about Comstock's height, willowy, red-haired, and instead of the dull apathetic look that most of our fellow citizens have, she has bright green eyes that penetrate right to the core of any problem. You'll know her as a fellow rebel as soon as you see her!"

Comstock wanted to ask how old she was but he couldn't. He felt that it might reveal the motives that were driving him out of the security of Bowdler's house into the harsh reality of his world, which he had grown to hate and fear.

Waving his hand in farewell to Bowdler, Helen and Grundy, he tried to look like one of the heroes he had been reading about. With that image in mind, he threw back his shoulders, took a deep breath, and slammed the door behind him. Then, head held high, he walked straight off the verandah and missed the top step completely.

Floundering, he landed in a heap at the bottom of the four steps.

It wasn't particularly heroic he feared, rising and brushing himself off.

Gulping, he walked out of sight of the enchanted house as quickly as he could. Ahead lay a world of danger, of familiar things that now were menacing and terrible.

But beckoning him on his way was a picture of a lovely red-haired, green-eyed girl who would fall languishing into his arms when he rescued her from the hands of the enemy.

Thinking about just what ways she would reveal her gratitude carried him along on seven league boots. As a matter of fact before he quite knew how he had covered the distance between the house and Puritan Square, he was there.

The streets were crowded with people but of a lovely red-haired siren there was no sign, no sign at all.

CHAPTER NINE

A WAVE of revulsion turned Comstock's stomach making him forget, for a moment, the girl for whom he was seeking. All around him in eddying mobs were elderly, grey and white haired women, their long dresses dragging on the ground. The idea that he had ever found them exciting was hard for him to bear. And the way the young men held the women's arms, talked to them, guided and protected them, made Comstock feel even queasier.

It was a Grandfather's Meeting night and all the couples were on their way to the meetinghouse. Above them all, the crazily careening green moon sent down harsh highlights that made the old women seem even more decrepit than they really were.

But search as Comstock would, of the red-haired girl he found no sign.

It was getting later and he saw an R.A.'s carriage come down the street, its astrobats dancing as the R.A. driver lashed them. He called out, "Nine o'clock, time for meeting!"

Knowing that he would be arrested if he stayed out on the street while everyone else went into the meetinghouse,

Comstock decided he had better try to look like a normal citizen. Even so, however, he was the recipient of an icy stare from the R.A. For he was the last person to enter the meeting place.

Comstock's flesh crawled when he found the last empty hard seat, and sat listening to the only too familiar smooth patter of the Elder who stood in the front of the hall, on a little podium and mouthed the old, only too familiar platitudes, about The Grandfather.

Closing his eyes, Comstock tried unavailingly to close his ears to the now meaningless words that flooded him and all the others in the crowded smelly meeting place.

The Elder was speaking, his seamed face hanging in lank folds, his jowls wobbling as they harked out the words, "And so, we know now that only in the lap of The Grandfather is there to be found the peace that passes all understanding…"

Comstock's eyes blinked open in shock when a clear, sweet voice interrupted the maunderings of the Elder by saying, "Poppycock!"

The Elder's face froze in ludicrous astonishment as he repeated after his heckler, "Poppycock?"

And then he saw her, Comstock did, and he was glad he hadn't murdered Grundy, and he was even gladder that his frozen tongue had not been able to utter words of love he had wanted to say to Helen. For he saw the girl for whom he had been searching and she was all his maddest dreams come true.

SHE stood up on her chair at one side of the hall and her eyes were as clear as Bowdler had said, and now they were flashing in anger. Her chest was heaving with indignation and Comstock found himself admiring the way her chest lent itself to this sort of treatment.

Waving one hand in the air for attention, she said, "You fools! How much longer are you going to be duped by the maunderings of these old fools? Don't you know that it's all a lie?"

The audience rose in its wrath and with one voice roared loudly enough to drown out all sounds that might have come from the girl.

The Elder, pointing a shaking arthritic forefinger at the girl, said in a feeble voice that didn't reach through the tumult. "She is insane. Call the R.A.'s."

But the crowd was too upset for any such normal proceedings. None of Comstock's reading had covered lynchings but that was the feeling that emanated from the furious people. This was a many-headed mob that wanted blood.

She was grabbed by so many hands that Comstock wondered if anything would be left of her. One man, bigger and stronger than the rest of the crowd roared out, "To the stocks with her!"

There was no way that Comstock could fight his way to her side, and even if he could have there was little he could have done but he attacked in his turn.

"The stocks," he kept thinking. They were outside in the square, just to one side of a statue of The Grandfather, where the graven image could look down in its infinite wisdom and be soothed and assuaged by the sight of its recalcitrant grandchildren being punished in the stocks.

If he waited, Comstock thought, till she was in them, there would be little he could do, for few ever lived through more than an hour of that treatment. The rocks and stones thrown by the good, lawful citizens of the community made sure of that.

No he could not wait, and yet what could he do as of that moment? What had possessed her to make her speak out in the meeting? The little fool. He'd shake some of the nonsense out of her, if he ever got her away from those menacing hands.

The crowd surged out of the meetinghouse, down the stairs and toward the statue. There was still no sign of any R.A. But then, why should there have been? Once everyone was at meeting, the R.A.'s could relax, having done their duty for the evening.

But how long could the rumble, the frightening mutter of all outraged mob continue before some R.A. heard it?

Comstock came to a sudden decision, as a ferocious and even more elderly woman than most reached forward and ripped the girl's dress from her neck to her navel, screeching, "The hussy! Put her in the stocks! I've got a stone for her! A big one perhaps one of you young sirs would help me throw it?" She looked about her coquettishly and her plea did not fall on empty air.

Running around the outer perimeter of the mob, Comstock made his way to the statue of the kindly faced Grandfather. Skirting the stocks, which were ugly and dull with the blood that had so many times defaced them, Comstock reached up and pulled himself into the lap of the stone Grandfather.

From that point of vantage he yelled, "Stop!"

His voice squeaked a little of course and did not come out with quite the roar that he had wanted it to, but it was enough, it served to halt the mob in its tracks.

Down below him, the girl, naked to the waist, her torn gown hanging from the belt that was all that retained the shreds of cloth that remained from the old woman's tearing hands, looked up at him.

The sight of her bare b+.....s was almost too much for Comstock. It unmanned him momentarily, but raising his eyes to her face, and seeing the courage that shone from her eyes, he recovered his lost voice and this time it came out with a roar, as he yelled, "Sanctuary! I claim the right of sanctuary for this girl and myself!"

IT had been over four hundred years since last a human voice had claimed that right. But in an ancestor directed culture like his, Comstock was sure that since old things were automatically the best things, his plea would *have* to be honored. Once having claimed sanctuary and while in the lap of the Grandfather, no one, not even the R.A. would tear you from that sacred place.

The mob was not at all happy, but it surrendered as he had been sure it would. The girl was passed up to him. His hands reaching down for her, were gladdened by the soft silkiness of her skin as he pulled her to him. Once she too was seated next to him in that broad capacious lap, the first thing she did, and he was sorry to see it happen, was to pull the shreds of her garment close around her.

Down below them the crowd was not silent. It looked up, and after a while its many faces merged into one, a fearful, frightening visage with one big voice that chanted, "You have sanctuary. We cannot deny you that. But sooner or later you must leave for you must eat and drink…and when you do…"

And when they did, Comstock knew, they'd be torn to shreds. For the anger, which formerly had been noisy and quarrelsome, was now quiet and, if anything, even more menacing than the noise had been.

But it would be a long time before he and the girl were forced to leave their sanctuary, and looking at her face, he decided that if he had to die, there were worse ways to go.

Shyly he put his hand out and stroked her flaming hair. Then he asked, "What's your name?"

"Patience and Fortitude Mather." She was still busy trying to arrange her torn clothing.

He gulped.

Noticing his surprise, she said, "But just call me Pat. What's your name?" Before he could answer she said, "Don't tell me you're a friend of…"

Nodding, he said, "Yes, I'm one of Bowdler's rebels." Then he identified himself.

"I should have known."

"Why," he asked with some asperity, "didn't you join us at Bowdler's house?"

"I couldn't shake off the R.A. who was following me and I wouldn't jeopardize the sanctum."

"Of course. But what made you decide to get up and carry on the way you did at the meeting?"

"When I finally did get away from the R.A. it was too late. It was past the time that Bowdler said I would be able to get through the force field. I knew I was lost and I decided I might just as well go down to defeat saying the things I'd always wanted to say."

"In case," Comstock said, "just in case, there is any chance of an escape from our present situation, and we should become separated..." and he told her about the two times of the day when it would be possible to get to Bowdler's house.

THE temperature went down as they sat on the cold stone and became acquainted. S+-x was the farthest thing from Comstock's mind when he moved closer to the girl and held her in his arms to try and preserve their mutual body heat. At least s+-x was far from his mind in the beginning of the long night. But as the evening hours wore away and the insane moon moved higher and higher in the sky, he found that hunger and thirst, cold and fear were not enough to keep certain thoughts from his now overheated brain. Just sitting so close to her was the most exciting experience he had ever had.

Below them the Hydra-head of the angry multitude began to murmur as he disregarded some of the conventions on which he had been raised. "Shameful," "Disgusting," "Perverted," "Horrible," were some of the milder epithets that were thrown through the air.

Her skin he found on investigation put any flower he had ever beheld to shame. Her breath was sweet on his nostrils. The feel of her was unlike anything he had ever dreamt of.

He said, his voice as low as his intentions, "Pat, do you think what I feel for you is love?"

Snuggling closer to him, she answered, "If it isn't, it's as good an imitation as we're likely to find." Then her inquisitive lips met his.

It was, he thought, even as he was experiencing it, a highly unlikely place in which to enjoy a honeymoon.

The shamelessness of their conduct was not lost on the waiting throng. At one point even the R.A. who had joined the mob and whose hand had never left the butt of his stun gun, found it necessary to walk away. None of the onlookers, as a matter of fact, could bear to watch.

So it was, that when Comstock accomplished his desire, and leaning back against The Grandfather's stony beard expressed some of his satisfaction by wishing he could fight the Board of Fathers, en masse, with one hand tied behind his back, he and Pat found that of the whole mob there was not a remnant.

Their conduct had shamed and frightened away the crowd.

Slipping down from the statue's lap, unable to believe their eyes, they skittered away in the now all-encompassing darkness, expecting at any moment to be halted by an R.A. or grabbed by some die-hards from the waiting crowd.

Jogging along at his beloved's side at a half-run, half-walk, Comstock wondered if even death could eradicate the exultation that he felt. But feeling as he did was not conducive, he found, to gloomy, dismal thoughts.

Not even when they ducked down a long alleyway, which he thought led in the general direction of Bowdler's house, did he really, deeply feel concerned about capture. Life could not be so unfair, he decided, as to raise him up to such heights as he had just surmounted, and then drop him into a gloomy pit.

But of course life could, and did, do just that.

CHAPTER TEN

HE could not help wonder as they ran through the alleyway towards a lighted area that might or might not lead to Bowdler's house, just how long the shock of what he had just done would keep the irate citizens off his trail. Pat ran at his side, her long legs easily keeping stride with him. If she was concerned about her own safety it did not show in her expression which was calm, and almost contemplative, if you disregarded the little quirk of a smile that turned up the ends of her full lips.

Despite the anxiety of his position, Comstock could not help but compare the feeling of ebullience and general physical well-being that surged through him, with the sadness and the feeling of despondency that he had always experienced after his monthly visits to the b+.....l.

If he had not been so busy running and praying that they could avoid the R.A.'s, he would like to have sat down and tried to reason out just what was the underlying reason for this change in his attitude towards sex, and its aftermath.

The pounding of their feet was the only sound in the silent night. Beside them the grey brick walls that lined the alley through which they ran were completely featureless. No windows or doors broke the long straight lines that reared up around them.

Pat paused and said, "Why are we running? It's quite clear that we..." she giggled, "scared everyone away with our outrageous conduct."

The fact that she was able to muster up a smile under these dire circumstances made a warm feeling well up in Comstock's chest. He feebly returned the smile, and then putting out his arms took her in them. He kissed her chastely on the lips and found that even this modest gesture made his temples pound.

Enfolding her and drawing her closer to him, he leaned his back against the nearest wall and whispered into her ear some of the phrases he had stored up from his reading which he had meant to say to Grundy's girl, Helen.

Their bodies were glued so tightly together that when the sound came, their start of surprise was completely mutual. "Ssssst." It sibilated. And then again, "Sssst!"

Thunderstruck, their arms still pressing around each other, Pat and Comstock looked around them. There was nothing to see. Nothing at all.

Then the sound became words, "Sssst, the R.A.'s after you?"

"Uh huh." Comstock managed to answer.

"Count three and then press against the fifth block from the ground."

Feeling that they had absolutely nothing to lose, Comstock obeyed the whispered command.

The fifth block up looked exactly like all the others. But when Comstock pushed at it, an irregular segment suddenly swung inwards. Low light was visible for a moment through the opening. Then it vanished and Comstock, holding Pat by the hand as though to give her reassurance, but really so that he could draw strength from her nearness, stepped through the dark aperture.

AT that particular moment, back at Bowdler's house, Grundy, Helen and the owner of the robot house were seated in the library. Bowdler had his hand outstretched to a lever that projected from behind some books. His eyes were glued to a clock. He said, "Five seconds...four...three..." then he shook his heavy head, and threw the lever back in its slot. "I'm afraid we'll have to give them up. It's past midnight. We'll try again at noon tomorrow."

"Don't you dare leave the force field open for a few moments more?" Grundy pleaded.

Shaking his leonine head, Bowdler pushed some books into place so that the lever was hidden from sight. "I would if I could, Grundy. But they must take their chances now."

"Even if Comstock has found that poor girl," Helen said, "what can they do out in the night?"

"Twelve more hours before they can make another attempt to reach safety here." Grundy shook his head. "I can't imagine where they can hide from the omnipresent R.A.'s."

"If only Comstock knew a little more," Helen said, "but we didn't dare try to open his eyes till you were here and it could be done under your aegis."

"The poor innocent," Bowdler said, "you were right to wait for me, but I wish things had worked out differently. Pat doesn't know much more about reality than Comstock." He sighed and then rested his big head on the myriad chins that formed a collar of flesh around his neck.

"What," Grundy asked, "will the R.A.'s do if they capture them?"

"Stun them to death, I'm afraid," Bowdler said.

"No," Helen said hopelessly, "no, they wouldn't…"

But the R.A.'s would, all three of them knew that. Then they just sat and waited, Bowdler staring sightlessly off into a future that only he could envisage, Helen and Grundy holding onto each other desperately in just the same fashion that Pat and Comstock were clinging to each other, as they followed someone or something through a pitch black room that seemed to stretch out forever.

THE peculiar door had swung to behind them making all seeing impossible. Comstock held his right arm around Pat's waist and held his left hand before him wishing that his fingertips could see.

The unknown voice that they had heard only once said, "Just a couple of seconds more, my buckos, and we'll be able to dispense with this blasted Stygian darkness."

A fumbling sound, a click, and then white light poured down in an iris-closing flood.

Blinking, Comstock and Pat looked around them. The room through which they had been moving sightlessly was big but not as big as their imaginations had made it. The clutter dwarfed the dimensions in any event. Every available foot of space ahead of them was piled high with a tangle of household objects that ranged from chairs and tables to rugs and bed linen.

Their mysterious host was facing them and as their eyes became accustomed to the light they saw a man of more than average height, lean as a willow branch, a piratical smile creasing his lantern jawed face, as he opened his arms in an all embracing gesture and said, "Welcome to the Haven."

Danger had made Comstock super-cautious, otherwise he might have ruined everything right then and there; for the first thought that occurred to him was that by some stroke of incalculable luck they had stumbled onto still another rebel. But remembering that Bowdler had said that there were only four fellow fighters altogether made Comstock wait for a lead. He said, "Thanks. You've probably saved our lives."

Hands on his narrow hips, the stranger frankly eyed Pat appreciatively. A low whistle preceded his next words, "Put twenty years on you, honey child, and you're going to be a real live doll!"

If this man liked old women, Comstock reasoned, he could not be a fellow rebel. But that made his conduct even more remarkable. Go slow, very slowly and carefully, Comstock brooded, as Pat smilingly asked, "May we know who you are?"

With vast mock-modesty, the man bowed low, and said, "I am known by a variety of names, none of them my own. I am perhaps best known as the Picaroon." Then he waited for them to express surprise and pleasure.

They just looked at him. Slightly crestfallen he rose from his bowing position, and said, almost anxiously, "You've heard of me? The Picaroon? I steal from the poor and give to the rich?"

Comstock turned his head and looked inquiringly at Pat. She was as puzzled as he.

Considerably crestfallen the man said, "The greatest outlaw in all New Australia? The man the R.A.'s would give their left arms to capture?" A frown crossed his face, then he said as though talking to himself, "The dirty nits! They were supposed to write me up, they promised they would, when I got sick and had to become a thief."

Whirling around on tiptoe like a dancer, he pointed at the accumulation of odds and ends that crowded the room. "Then what have I been working so hard for? Why have I worked my fingers to the bone stealing...stealing, out every night when I should be asleep, burglarizing every innocent house I come to? Why, I ask you, why? It's enough to make a man become a cynic, that's what it is!"

Slumping into a chair that was already overcrowded with various objects, he put his head in his hands. A terrifying thought seemed to occur to him. He looked up at them. "If you don't even know who I am, if they aren't even writing up my criminal exploits, what did I go to all the trouble of preparing this Haven for? If they're not chasing me, if there is no danger, how can my cure work?"

"I'm sure I don't know," Comstock said since the man seemed to want some kind of an answer. All the while the thief had been talking, Comstock had been racking his weary brain trying to recollect what illness crime was a cure for. He couldn't remember.

A hopeful look came over the man's face and he leaped up from his seat. A long forefinger jutted out at Comstock. The man said, "I've got it. You're lying to me! You're undercover workers for the R.A. You're spies come to root me out! Luckily I have taken precautions against that very thing. The Picaroon can't be caught napping! No indeed!"

Whirling around the man who called himself the Picaroon suddenly swooped towards a pile of metallic looking objects whose identity Comstock had not yet been able to determine.

The thing he grabbed was about three feet long, made of some shining metal, was about an inch in diameter and came to a point. The handle, if that was what it was, glittered as he inserted his hand in the metallic basketwork and twirled the point of the object dangerously near Comstock's nose. Comstock felt his nostrils twitch as the object stirred up a breeze as it swirled past him.

The lean man said, "I knew this old sword would come in handy some day. No one can outwit the Picaroon." He laughed and his voice was pitched at what Comstock considered an almost hysterical note.

The point of what the Picaroon had called a sword swung back and forth in front of Pat and Comstock. With his other hand he grabbed a long loop of narrow cloth and threw it to Pat. "Tie up your fellow spy and then I'll take care of you…"

Comstock said, "Do as he tells you, Pat, darling. Do it instantly." His voice quavered for he had suddenly recollected what sickness it was that thieving cured.

Unexpectedly docile, Pat did as she was directed. She tied Comstock's hands behind his back, not too tightly, however, Comstock was pleased to notice, and then turning, faced their captor.

She asked, "What now, noble Picaroon?"

"Good girl," Comstock thought. "She's realized that only madmen are forced to become anti-social creatures."

Humming to himself the Picaroon whirled the point of the "sword" under Comstock's chin and said to Pat, "If only you were a little older, child, you and I could make such beautiful music together... But then there's no reason why I can't keep you here in the Haven till you age properly, now is there?"

"No," Pat agreed hastily, "none at all."

The lunatic whistled cheerily to himself as he cleared a free space on a couch and forced Pat to lie down on it. Then he tied her ankles with a silk scarf, and her wrists with a plastic substance that was known to have a tensile strength equal to that of the metal that this culture used for the framework of their buildings.

Donning a broad brimmed hat, and throwing a cape-like cloth around his wide shoulders, the Picaroon bowed deeply to Pat. Walking to one wall, he pressed his fingers against a projecting button and said, "'Tis not long past midnight...there's a bad night's work still to be done. Tonight, the Picaroon strikes again!"

HE was gone. They were alone. Comstock looked helplessly at Pat. She tried to manufacture a smile but it was no great shakes.

"If," Comstock said, "I can get this thing off my wrists, perhaps we can be out of here before that insane creature returns."

"Escape from this retreat directly into the Grandfather's Right Arms?" Pat asked gently.

Comstock stopped struggling with his bonds for a moment as he considered what she had said. "If we can fend off this 'Picaroon' until about eleven-thirty tomorrow then we can make a dash for Bowdler's house.

"I think that's our only chance, and a slim one it is."

Almost twelve hours ahead of them, at the mercy of a madman, before they could dare run the daylight gauntlet of the outdoors, under the menace of the R.A.'s. Comstock shuddered. The risk was tremendous, yet what else was there that they could do? He couldn't bear the thought of staying here in the Picaroon's Haven right around the clock, he didn't think he could stand twenty-four hours more of the nerve racking strain he was undergoing, even though that might be a more intelligent plan to attack.

Roughly twelve hours more, one way, and a full twenty-four the other...

Pat said, when she saw his brow furrowed with painful thought. "Now's the time to think of my name."

"Huh?" he said, not very intelligently.

"Patience and Fortitude, remember?"

He had the patience, the only question was whether or not he had the fortitude to put up with the Picaroon's mad fantasies.

At length the secret door opened and the man he was brooding about entered, bowed down with an even more useless collection of stolen objects than the ones that already burdened the room.

Striking an attitude, the Picaroon dropped the load he was carrying and roared, "Once more has the Picaroon dared the armed forces and the majesty of The Grandfather's law; once more his nimble fingers have plucked from the very heart of our solid citizenry those stolen treasures which will emblazon his name in the criminal hall of fame."

He bowed.

Pat said under her breath, "Patience and Fortitude..."

Then the Picaroon darted suddenly towards Comstock, his lean fingers outstretched. He said, "And you, you poisonous emissary of the forces of law and order, you, the Picaroon will punish in fitting style!"

Comstock held his breath as he waited to see what new vagary had further addled the brain of their insane captor.

CHAPTER ELEVEN

BEFORE the Picaroon's fingers had quite tightened around Comstock's throat, Pat called out, "Perhaps there is some good reason why your exploits have not been emblazoned for all to read?"

The strong fingers slowly opened and the madman turned towards Pat.

Taking the cue, Comstock said hurriedly, "Yes, maybe your crimes have not been particularly spectacular?" Some place in Bowdler's huge library Comstock had run across a book devoted to the exploits of a super criminal. Rummaging through his memory, Comstock said, "I've got it! I know just the thing that the Picaroon can do that will insure his infamy becoming noticed."

As Pat began to speak, the Picaroon's head swiveled back and forth between her and Comstock. His steel grey eyes were no longer menacing, Comstock was pleased to note.

"How about," Pat suggested, "how about stealing..."

"One of the R.A.'s cars," Comstock interjected.

"Just what I was going to say. And then with the aid of the car, he can..."

"Go to the fountainhead, beard The Grandfather in his retreat."

"And make sure that his most fantastic and fabulous crime will become known to every living creature in our world by..."

"Snipping off The Grandfather's beard!" Comstock finished. Then he waited, his teeth pressed together on his bottom lip.

"But," the Picaroon said, in a rather bemused fashion, "that would be blasphemy."

172

"But think of the effrontery of it?" Pat said, leaning forward hopefully, paying no attention to the bonds that held her.

"Think of the shock of such an action! Every law-abiding citizen would rise up in wrath. Then the hue and cry would be such that no longer would the Picaroon work long hard hours through the night without ever getting the fame which is his due." Comstock could hardly believe that even this lunatic would fall for what they were suggesting.

"What a colossal feat..." the Picaroon said, almost to himself, "Why didn't *I* think of it?"

His long legs carried him around the room, as unthinkingly, he strode up and down over the various bundles that were strewn around the floor.

A thought struck the man who called himself the Picaroon. "Where could we steal an R.A.'s car?"

This, of course, was the crux of Comstock's plan. Looking as unconcerned as he could. Comstock said. "Why, it just happens that Pat and I know where there is an abandoned car."

"An abandoned car?" The Picaroon grinned delightedly, snapped his fingers and said, "Then come, the night is young and there is dirty work to be done!" Running to Pat's side he released her. She rose, rubbed her fingers to restore the circulation and then untied Comstock.

Comstock eyed her torn dress, the involuntary deshabille that revealed more of her firm young b+.....s than he thought any other man in the world should be in a position to observe and said to the Picaroon, "Remember, this is a most dangerous adventure on which we are about to embark. We are wanted as badly by the R.A.'s as you will be once you have snipped off The Grandfather's beard! We'd best wear some disguise."

"Then," the Picaroon said, "You two are really not police spies at all, are you?"

"Wait and see what the R.A.'s do to us if they catch us," Pat said grimly, while she rooted through a rag bag of old clothes trying to find some sort of garment with which to clothe herself.

"How exciting," the Picaroon said, slapping his hands together in delight, "and to think I was just about to crown my criminal career by murdering this man."

Comstock tried not to think about how close his demise had been and watched fascinatedly while Pat dropped her torn dress to the floor and donned a shapeless gown.

But when he saw the Picaroon was busy searching for male clothes he turned away from the delectable sight of Pat's n+..e body and took the clothes that the Picaroon gave him. A floppy hat had a big enough brim so that in the dark Comstock's face would be hidden. A tight pair of trousers and a too big jacket of a different color than the things he had been wearing would have to suffice as a disguise. All Comstock could do really, was hope and pray that they would be able to get, with the Picaroon's aid, near enough to Bowdler's house so that while the Picaroon was busy trying to understand the mechanics of the abandoned car, he and Pat could make a run for it through the force field at the proper time.

THE trip through the darkened city was a revelation to both Pat and Comstock. In Comstock's earlier, law-abiding incarnation, there had never been a night that found him in bed later than the curfew at ten. To find that the streets were completely deserted at two, or three o'clock in the morning came as no surprise, since he knew that all lawful souls would, of course, be asleep at that time.

But he had not been an alcoholic for a long enough period to find out that the bars stayed open long after midnight. The only people that there was the slightest chance of trouble with, were the roisterers who staggered out of the saloons from time to time, and here the danger was slight, for as soon as an inebriate hove into view the Picaroon would wink mightily, link arms with Pat on one side and with Comstock on the other and the trio would mimic drunkenness and sing bawdy songs till the real drunks were gone.

"What," Comstock asked, "are the chances of bumping into an R.A.?"

"Aha!" The Picaroon placed his long forefinger next to his nose. "You are attempting to tear aside the veil that hides the Picaroon's methods!"

"Fiddle faddle," Pat said nastily, "answer him!"

Coming to a halt on a silent street corner under a lamppost that cast a spotlight down around his piratical figure, the Picaroon said, "At night, after curfew, when all law-abiding citizens sleep..." He lowered his voice to a shadow of a whisper forcing Pat and Comstock to place their ears near his mouth, "you realize, don't you, both of you, that I am giving away my most cherished secret, the modus operandi that allows me to operate and so flout the law?"

They nodded.

"Then let it be known, but just to us, that I have found when all the other law-abiding citizens sleep, why, so do the R.A.'s."

Twirling in a mad pirouette, the Picaroon threw back his head and laughed. "From curfew to dawn, there is no law!"

Clapping a hand over the Picaroon's mouth, Comstock snapped, "Shut up! You'll rouse the dead with all that noise!"

A little sobered the Picaroon said, "Now you have my most valued secret, see that you guard it with your lives!" Putting his finger to his lips he added, "Hisssst..."

Pat asked, "What is it?"

"Nothing," the Picaroon said, "I just like to say hisssst..."

Shrugging behind the Picaroon's back, Comstock gestured to Pat to pay no mind to their mad guide. Aloud, he asked, "Do you know your way to 14 Anthony Comstock Road?"

"I know all the ways," The Picaroon said, and again taking the lead, walked with exaggerated steps, on tiptoe, as though fearing to wake the sleeping world.

It was a long trip on foot and dawn was breaking as they came in sight of some landmarks that Comstock remembered. If his mental picture of the terrain was correct, the car in which Grundy, Helen and he had made their escape from the Fathers should be downhill from where he and Pat and the Picaroon were now standing.

He conveyed this information to the others and this time he took the lead with Pat behind him and the Picaroon still walking on tiptoe bringing up the rear.

As they went downhill Comstock could see his goal. Bowdler's house lay still and quiet, the refuge for which he yearned. But it might just as well have been on the other side of his world for all the good it was as long as the force field surrounded it.

Waiting till the Picaroon's attention was on the car in the distance, Comstock pointed at the house and whispered to Pat, "That's it."

She nodded.

Then they reached the car and the Picaroon's almost idiot glee reached its apogee as he poked at the thing under the hood that made the "car" move.

Comstock didn't have the vaguest idea of whether or not the car could run. When he and Grundy and Helen had abandoned it, it had simply gone careening downhill and finally stopped. Why it stopped, or whether it would ever go again was an impenetrable question to Comstock.

But he didn't allow his lack of knowledge to stand in his way. Becoming dictatorial he told the Picaroon to stop fooling about with the mechanism and to watch and try to learn how to make the car go.

Then with the Picaroon standing at attention, Comstock got into the car, and went through the complex series of actions, which in Grundy's case had served to animate the vehicle.

There was a muttering rumble from the "car" and it surged internally. However the rock which had halted its forward progress in the first place, still served to prevent it from proceeding.

THE Picaroon snapped into action, and going to the rear of the "car" he pushed as the wheels of the vehicle began to spin to no avail, at all.

At this point, Comstock, anxious to stall things as long as he could, since there was no chance of entering Bowdler's house till the sun was overhead, tried to turn off the motor. Instead he threw the motor into reverse and the car instantly backed up, carrying the Picaroon along with it.

He dangled from the rear of the car trying to muscle himself up out of the danger of the wheels while he yelled at the top of his lungs for Comstock to stop whatever he was doing.

Pat sat on the side of the road being of no help to Comstock at all, since she was busy being convulsed by giggles. The sight of the long-legged madman, his no longer jaunty cape entangled in his thrashing limbs, while Comstock wildly snapped things on and off on the control board, and the unguided car veered and yawed as it ran backwards up the steep hill was a little more than she could stand.

When the car had backed almost to the crest of the hill, Comstock found the key, which turned the ignition on and off and managed to bring the "car" to a halt.

The Picaroon was in a towering fury. "Poltroon!" he roared at Comstock who was red-faced with embarrassment and anxiety. "How dare you treat a criminal figure of my stature in a manner more befitting some low comedy person like you?"

Dropping from the rear of the "car" the Picaroon raced around towards the driving wheel where Comstock sat helplessly trying to deduce what had gone wrong with his method of driving the "car".

The Picaroon's right hand darted out of sight under his cape and when it came back into view, Comstock was horrified to see that a steel blade perhaps ten inches long had become integral to the maniac's right hand.

"Blood," the Picaroon stated almost calmly, "blood is the only thing that will erase this stain that you have placed on my criminal escutcheon."

With that he darted the sharp point of the knife straight at what would have been Comstock's Adam's apple, had not a beginning double chin covered it with fat.

There is no doubt that Comstock would have died at the wheel of the car, with a slit throat had not Pat, seeing the direction that the madman's mind was taking, picked up a rock and smashed it down on the Picaroon's head just in the only too well known nick of time.

Breath whooshed out of Comstock's lungs as he saw the knife blade falter, and then saw the Picaroon's head come careening down.   Wide-eyed he watched as the man's unconscious body tumbled to the ground.

As soon as the Picaroon landed, Pat was at his side and her questing hand first took the knife from his flaccid grip and then she examined the rest of the arsenal that hung from the man's belt hidden till now by the all-encompassing cloth of his ridiculous cape.

The plethora of weapons clinked and clanked as she placed them to one side. She said, "When you get your breath, come and take some of these for yourself, dear."

COMSTOCK found that if he didn't pay too much attention to the way his knees wobbled that he could navigate. Getting out of the car was hardest. Once he was on firm ground again he found that the various alarums and excursions through which he had lived had served to, if not make him callous to danger, at least make him bounce back a little faster than he had at the beginning of his departure from his normal way of life.

Holding his right forefinger on his left pulse for a moment he wondered why his poor weak heart had not long ago surrendered beneath the various assaults that had been made on it. But when he found that his pulse seemed to be practically normal he forgot about his heart until kneeling down next to Pat he smelled the fragrance of her hair. This time he did not have to take his pulse. He could feel his heart pounding.

She looked sideways at him and smiled gently. They were both kneeling next to the prostrate Picaroon. Their mouths were on a level. This made their kissing almost automatic.

The kiss might have lasted even longer than it did had not the Picaroon stirred. Pat broke away from Comstock's embrace and said, "We'd best tie him up so that we don't have any more trouble with him."

"By all means," Comstock said muzzily, his mind still concerned with the nearness of her.

It was only when she rose and went to the car looking for something with which to bind their captive that Comstock was able to think, shake his head and force his addled brain into action again.

Then using the cape as a blanket, Comstock swathed the madman in its folds. Next, when Pat returned with some rope they wound it around and around the man till he was completely bound.

Then, and only then, did Comstock turn and look across the distance that separated them from Bowdler's house and safety. The sun was well up now, which was good in that it shortened their waiting time, but was bad since it meant that the R.A.'s would be out on patrol in full force.

Pat, standing at his side, voiced his thoughts when she said, "Isn't there some way that we could signal to your friends so that we need not wait out here till noon?"

"The big danger to be avoided is that the R.A.'s may see us and so suspect the house."

Below them, the Picaroon rolled his head back and forth angrily. This was the only part of him that he could move. He said, "So you *were* spies!" he spat. "I should have known. Always should the master criminal work alone. All the textbooks I have read make that point. It serves me right for not being a lone mink…or wolf or whatever the earth word is."

Comstock paid no attention to his grumbling as he tried to assay the situation. They could not endanger the safety of the house by just walking into view of one of the windows and waving to capture the attention of Grundy or Helen.

If an R.A. were to see that…

Since that was impossible, what were their chances of being unobserved for...looking up at the sun he tried to estimate how long it would be before noon. Perhaps two hours yet.

Putting his arm around Pat's waist he said, "Let's get as close to the force field as we can so that when it is lifted we can just make a dash for the house."

"And take a chance of being seen by an R.A.?"

That was right. When Bowdler told him to come back to the house at noon or midnight, he had had no way of knowing just how badly the R.A.'s would be wanting to get hold of Pat and Comstock. It hardly seemed possible to Comstock that so little time had passed since he had left the house and safety the day before to go hunting for an unknown girl.

He gulped as he realized what the tenor of his thinking meant. He said plaintively, "You mean we'll have to wait till midnight before we dare go to the house?"

She nodded.

Then, as one person they turned and looked down at the Picaroon. It would be unfair to keep the poor lunatic tied up the way he was for at least fourteen more hours...

The Picaroon was mumbling to himself, "You are who you are, if you think you are..."

Blinking thoughtfully, Comstock turned to Pat and said, "You know, that's a very interesting question. I'd like to think about it for a while."

"While you're thinking about it, darling, devote a little of your brain power to figuring out where we're going to get food and water to last us till midnight..."

The madman's words pounded at Comstock's brain washing away the reality of what the girl had said. "But how do you know you are?" That was a very interesting question.

Still squatting on his heels, Comstock looked unseeingly off into the distance and wondered what in the name of The Grandfather the answer to the lunatic's question could be.

He was something or someone called Comstock, he was sure of that. But how could he know he was Comstock, for sure, that is?

He was so engrossed that he did not even hear the Picaroon's mad giggle as the man said to Pat, "See…see what my little question did to him? That's what happened to the first four doctors who examined me!" He laughed again. "That was when the Fathers decided that I was a madman and that my only cure was to become a criminal."

Worry made itself visible on Pat's face as she turned from looking at Comstock who was completely withdrawn inside himself. She looked down at their captive and asked, "Who were you before you became the Picaroon?"

The harsh piratical face lost its Harlequinesque self-derision as the man said, "I was the last philosopher."

CHAPTER TWELVE

THERE was something so infinitely sad in the man's words that Pat was emotionally moved. Not knowing what a philosopher might be did not prevent her from feeling sorry that the bound man had been the last of whatever it was that he had been.

Comstock never knew about the conversation that the quondam Picaroon had with Pat, for all the while that the girl and the bound man talked, Comstock was in a little world of his own trying to chase down the reality of his own existence.

Sitting on the ground next to the man who called himself the Picaroon and the last philosopher, Pat found herself involved in a discussion of what the man spoke of as the eternal verities.

The sun rose higher and higher in the sky, noon came and went while Comstock went deeper and deeper into himself searching for the answer that does not exist.

When he had not moved for many hours, Pat tore herself away from what she was being told and asked, "What can I do for him?"

For the first time in many hours the philosopher gave place to the Picaroon and the madman, laughing gleefully as he said, "All you need do is find the answer for which he is questing. That will bring him out of the grey world into which the question has driven him."

Looking at Comstock, Pat felt fear like a live thing. There was no intelligence on his soft face. None at all. His eyes were unfocussed, his breathing very slow. His arms were hooked around his knees, which were drawn up towards his chest. He had fallen over on his side.

Luckily Pat had no idea of what the fetal position looks like or she would have been even more frightened than she was.

Pat asked hesitantly. "Will you tell me the answer so that I can help him come back?"

Then the madman threw his lean face back and howled.

Wringing her hands, Pat wondered what had come over the man who such a short time before had told her wonderful things of which she had never dreamed.

When he was strangling with his own mirth, the man gasped, "My dear, I would gladly give the answer...that's what I devoted all my life to searching for...but the humor of it all is that there is no answer."

Then another paroxysm of laughter swept through him.

Deep down inside Comstock's brain in the never-never land to which the last philosopher's question had driven him, Comstock was dully aware that his body was being stroked. It felt nice and he made an animal sound deep in his throat. But the action did not serve to revive him any more than Pat's anxious voice, which was shouting in his unhearing ears.

He never heard her say, "Darling, you *must* come back! The R.A.'s are coming."

Comstock never knew when a squad of R.A.'s surrounded the car, and by means of a frightening array of stun guns forced Pat to help them carry first the tied-up lunatic and then the unresisting body of the man she loved into the car in which they had driven onto the scene.

INSIDE Bowdler's house Grundy, Helen and the owner of the robot house sighed as midnight came and went. Bowdler voiced all their feelings when he said, "I am afraid we must give them up for lost. We have waited through three periods. There has been no sign of them. None at all."

While he was saying this, the R.A.'s were driving away with Comstock, Pat and the Picaroon.

"Then we can wait no longer?" Helen asked.

Shaking his head, Bowdler said, "No."

Grundy rose to his feet as he murmured. "I'm glad. This waiting has been worse than anything that the Board of Fathers can mete out to us."

Helen and Grundy paused at the door of the house and looked back regretfully, Grundy spoke, "It's been a wonderful month we had, we can remember that, darling."

She kissed him and they walked out into the darkness with Bowdler close behind them.

He said, "I shall be with you, and you can depend on my helping in any way that I can."

"To face the Board of Fathers!" Grundy's face was set, "I'll tell them a few home truths no matter what they finally decide to do to us."

"You're so brave, sweetheart," Helen said. And looked at him admiringly.

"But it's still The Grandfather whom I fear the most." Grundy was honest enough to add.

Bowdler laid his heavy hands on each of them and said, "Courage."

Then they started on the way to their fates.

IN the R.A.'s car, Pat sat between the lump of unresisting flesh that Comstock had become and the cocoon-like figure of the philosopher.

The man who was a criminal in spite of himself observed the way Pat looked down at Comstock and his harshly handsome face softened.

"My dear, perhaps it is better that he be the way he is, if what you have told me is true and you are both rebels against the bonds that chain all of us on this sorry world of ours. I fear what the Board of Fathers or The Grandfather may decide may be much worse than this condition that my question has caused."

"To die is hard, but to die without knowing that you are dying, is horrible," Pat said through clenched teeth.

"It is unmanly, I will not gainsay that." Then the man was silent.

Ahead of them the odd buildings that housed the Board and The Grandfather rose up in their way. The globular buildings inside of which were both the Elders and the Fathers were dwarfed by the height of the shaft of The Grandfather's residence.

The R.A.'s were as silent and seemingly unthinking as machines. Their first visible emotion had been one of jubilance at having caught Pat and Comstock but that had faded under the fear of punishment for not having caught them sooner.

They sat statue still, their hands on their guns as the car drove up to the entrance of the buildings.

One of the R.A.'s left the machine to go for further orders from his superior officer.

In the car the last philosopher said softly, "Perhaps whatever little nobility there is in man is best served by dying with one's eyes open. I shall not again retreat into the lie of the Picaroon." He smiled gently at Pat, and said, "I think I will like dying as one of you, as a rebel."

But all Pat's attention was on her beloved who had never stirred from the curled up position into which his thoughts had forced him.

Seeing this, the last philosopher said, "There is one chance, and only one that I can think of that may revive him. Perhaps love, an emotion of which I know very little, may be strong enough to pull him out of that place to which he has run for safety."

"What do you mean?" she asked.

"To me," the man said, "as a philosopher, the charms of love and sex were never very strong. But I should imagine, just as pure speculation, that the two must be very tightly entwined."

Deep, deep down inside the thing that Comstock had become he felt a stirring of some kind of interest. He did not yet know what was causing the sensation, he could not hear the love words that Pat was whispering in his ear, he was not really conscious of her soft hands caressing him, but something was taking place, something that seemed to have reality in a place where there was no such thing.

SO it was that the guards of the R.A. were as shocked by her behavior as earlier the waiting crowd had been when Comstock and Pat had broken the deepest, strongest held taboo of their culture.

At their side, the last philosopher chuckled as he saw the guards blanch, then turn their eyes away.

Their livid faces were turned from the scene as Pat literally drew Comstock back from the bourne to which he had retreated.

Gasping, astounded, Comstock came back to reality. He was terribly shocked when he saw what Pat had done, but this shock gave place to an even bigger one when he realized that they had been captured, that they were in front of The Grandfather's Retreat, and that there was no longer any chance for escape.

None at all.

Gasping, he asked, "What happened? Where have I been? How did we get here? Why don't I remember coming here?"

"Don't repeat my question," the last philosopher said, "or he may be trapped by it again."

Slurring over the crux of the matter, Pat gently tried to bring Comstock up to date.

The guards recovered some of their equanimity and brutally shoved all three of them out of the car. The last philosopher, still bound, crashed to his face as they evicted him. Pat hurried to untie him and help him to his feet.

Then, inside a living square formed by the R.A.'s they were ushered back into the anteroom which Comstock, Grundy and Helen had escaped from a month earlier.

Surprise was piled on surprise for Comstock. When the R.A.'s shoved him into the room he saw, waiting, sitting in chairs, Helen and Grundy. Standing, pacing back and forth was Bowdler, his heavy face set with thought.

Helen cried, "We thought you were dead!"

Then there were introductions, and explanations, and it was only quiet when Bowdler finally interrupted and said, "Hold everything. You realize it is late at night, and it is only because of the uniqueness of the situation that the Board of Fathers is sitting in extraordinary session—in order to decide what to do with you all—that I am here."

This sufficed to let Comstock and Pat know that Bowdler was still playing his double game.

Helen whispered in Comstock's ear. "Bowdler pretended that he had captured us and brought us here and then invoked the special session of the Fathers."

Just as the door that led into the Board of Fathers began to open, Bowdler said, his voice harsh with urgency, "I want you to go in there, not as prisoners come to judgment, but as stalwarts who demand a fitting place in the government of our world.

"Audacity, my little ones, audacity is the order of the day!" Bowdler smiled as he saw the puzzlement spread over Comstock's and Pat's faces. "Follow the lead of Grundy and Helen. I've had time to tell them a little more than I have told you two."

The door was open wide now, and as Comstock girded his loins preparatory to what he was sure would be a battle to the death against impossible odds, the R.A. who had entered, bowed to Bowdler and said, "The Fathers request your presence, Father Bowdler."

Then their last prop was gone, and they just sat and waited, staring at the door which had closed behind Bowdler.

THE three who had endured so much sat and waited. The three plus Pat and the last philosopher. When you have fought for as long as they had against forces strong almost beyond imagining, when you have struggled in despair, lived without daring to think, hope, when it finally comes is almost anti-climactic. At least Comstock found it so. Despite the traps, the violence, the hurts, the fear, they were now where they wanted to be.

They sat quietly, their hands folded, and if any feeling of triumph was in them, it was so muted as not to be observable. At that precise moment, when they sat in the anteroom, waiting for their reward, if reward it were to be, the only common emotion they shared was that they had fought a good fight. Fought as hard as it is in a person to fight for what they consider right.

Then the door opened and instead of the summons to come before the Board of Fathers, which they had expected, The Grandfather entered the room. The Grandfather, with his high hooked nose, his broad forehead, deep set harsh old blue eyes, focused on the middle distance, his strong old hands crossed on his stomach just below his patriarchal beard, his tremendous height forcing him to look down at them.

It was hard to believe.

Hard to believe that they, or anyone below the rank of Father would ever actually behold Him in the flesh.

When He spoke His voice was all the things they had known it would be... Deep as an organ base, calm, full of authority, stern, yet with a leavening of those other things that make up the whole man, his voice was almost gentle as he said, "Follow me, please."

They rose, and feeling like little children, followed his preposterously tall, spare back, out of the anteroom, into that other room where the Board awaited them.

There was no fear in them now as there would have been earlier. For they were not coming before the Board for judgement, but to be rewarded. At least that's what Grundy and Helen had been told by Bowdler.

The Grandfather pointed out Comstock, Helen and Grundy, and said, "These three are the original ones. The other two," his gesture pointed out the last philosopher and Pat, "are the newer recruits."

There was silence.

"They have come to join us," The Grandfather said.

The silence expanded.

"Gentlemen, Fathers all, these are three new Fathers." The Grandfather's voice faded away and there was no other sound. Some of the men who made up the Board of Fathers said a word, but the ones who had fought their way up to this eminence stood in silence and looking about them, examined the men with whom they would now share the control of their whole world.

This was the moment of their triumph.

CHAPTER THIRTEEN

WHEN Bowdler and Grundy had first sounded out Comstock and had asked him the questions that had led him so far from the normal law-abiding life that had been his, one of the mainsprings of his conduct had been envy mixed with disgust that the Fathers whom formerly he had so revered had become monsters in his mind. Monsters who had used the whole planet as a breeding ground for their harems. For when the thought that only the Fathers were really fathers had struck Comstock he had resolved that he too would like to take part in such noble work.

Along with the sexual motive, Comstock had decided that if the Fathers controlled the world, he too would like to have a share in either controlling the world as it was, or perhaps with luck, helping to change the control in such a way that their world would be a better place to live in.

This mixture of ideas had resulted in his mental picture of the Fathers becoming an amalgam of monsters of pride, venery and power.

Looking about the room Comstock decided that he could not possibly have been further wrong in the way he had pictured the Fathers.

For his first feeling as his unbelieving eyes swept around the table at which the Fathers sat, was one of pity.

Far from being the creatures with inflated egos, the monsters of uxoriousness that his inflamed imagination had painted, these men who guided the affairs of his world were invalids... The lame, the halt and the blind.

Each face was torn by pain, every body bore the stigmata of some fatal disease.

Only the Grandfather, ridiculously tall and spare, standing at the far end of the gigantic room was as his imagination had foretold He would be.

In the silence that greeted them Comstock finally turned to Grundy and said, "I...I don't understand."

The Grandfather walked to the head of the table and prepared to speak. While they waited, Grundy whispered, "Think a moment. The only cure for disease that our people know is vice. Right?"

Nodding, Comstock waited.

"But the only people on the whole planet who know how this cure works, what psychic machinery is involved, are the Fathers."

Comstock gulped and thought of his heart.

"To become a Father," Grundy added hurriedly as The Grandfather raised his hand for silence, "is a sentence of death.

For once you know how sin cures sickness, it can no longer cure you."

"Fathers," The Grandfather said, and involuntarily, Comstock felt his heart fill with awe, so imbued had his upbringing been with respect and worship of the figure called The Grandfather; he tried to control the emotion that threatened to unman him, for his temptation was to fall down before The Grandfather.

"Fathers," the deep organ bass went on, "you know why we are gathered in this extraordinary conclave. So successful has been the regime that I have caused to come into being, that no longer can we hope to recruit new Fathers from amongst those brave souls who rebel against the government we have set up. Not for fifty years has a new rebel appeared to challenge our power. Therefore, as you all know, Father Bowdler, because he is the healthiest appearing of any of you, was empowered to go out into the world and find rebellious souls whom we may be able to use as leaders.

"I feared when first I caused the apparatus of power to be set up as I have done, that there would be instant and successful rebellion. It did not then occur to me that I would be too successful and that rebellion would be bred out of the blood of our people.

"We have, as you know only too well, arrived at a period of stasis from which our world may never recover.

"It therefore devolves upon the men who stand before you as well as the women who have made common cause with them, to come to our aid.

"Now that aid is to be given, what these new Fathers will be able to do before death claims them, I do not know. All that I can say with any assurance, is that if something is not done and done quickly, our world will go down the road to static death, never knowing what has toppled it from the high estate it held."

COMSTOCK'S mind was almost incapable of digesting what The Grandfather was saying. It had all happened much too quickly. To be raised in a matter of moments from a position where death seemed imminent first to a position on the Board of Fathers, and now, if he understood correctly, to be told that the future of the world was somehow his responsibility, was just too much.

His first instinctual response was to desire escape. Turning around he saw directly behind him, a door that was ajar. Not that he wanted to escape very far, he just wanted to go off in a dark corner and sit and think the whole thing out.

The Grandfather was still speaking, as Comstock, unobserved, began to step backwards. The others, Comstock's fellow rebels were leaning forward, greedily drinking in what The Grandfather was saying.

"You will, in the next day or two," The Grandfather was saying as Comstock backed closer to the door, "be told just how our government operates. You will be told how, when the last scientists were martyred by an unreasoning mob, they tried, before death claimed them, in their wisdom to set up non-mechanical devices that would cure the sick. They knew that in the period of dark reaction by which they were swept to death, anything that smelled of machinery was doomed to destruction.

"You will then understand why I was in effect forced to cause this world of ours to enter a period of the strictest moral upbringing. Only under such a regime could the psychosomatic mechanisms that the scientists had explained, be able to work.

"I have been only too successful as you know. I have, by the restrictions I set up, brought into being a world where people fear sickness not because of the pain it brings, but because of the shame the sins which cure it bring in its path."

Then the door was near enough so that Comstock was able to duck through it. There was a hard bench just outside and as Comstock sat down on it, his brain awhirl, he heard the deep voice of The Grandfather say, just as Comstock pushed the door closed, "But enough of the way our world works now. I think the next subject under discussion will be just what we can do to make our world take the step from an inner-directed culture with ancestor-directed overtones, on and up to the next normal step which is an other-directed culture."

INASMUCH as the last thing that Comstock remembered clearly was when he brought the "car" under control and then tied up the man he knew as the Picaroon, he sat on the hard bench, his buttock muscles sore from lack of sleep, his stomach gurgling loudly from lack of food and water, and tried to reconstruct just what had been happening to him.

It was no use. There was a lapse he could not account for. He remembered that the Picaroon had asked him a question, but luckily he could not remember how it was phrased, and then the next thing he knew he was getting out of the R.A.'s car, being guided into the fearful sanctum of the Fathers, and then, first fearing instant death, he had then been apprised of his accession to power. Then the membership of the Board of Fathers had been revealed to be a sentence of death, and before his weary, battered brain could recover from that, The Grandfather had made it clear that the world's future was somehow his responsibility.

Comstock was only too aware of his mortality, as everyone is when fatigue has lowered one's defenses. He slouched down on the bench and tried to rationalize some of the recent events.

Aside from Pat, he would be only too grateful if the whole benighted affair had never been and he could once more awaken in bed with his mother near to comfort him.

The door on the far side of the room opened and an R.A. entered. Comstock was sunk too far down in a welter of self-pity to do more than raise his head tiredly and look at the R.A.'s stern face. The uniformed man produced a stun gun and said, "You are under arrest."

Before Comstock could bother to tell the man that he was a little behind in his knowledge of what had been happening. the gun did its work.

Stunned, Comstock fell off the bench and crashed onto the floor. His head landed so hard that the result was instant unconsciousness. The effect of the gun's energy bolt would merely have been to immobilize his bodily functions. But the blow knocked him out.

WHEN he opened his eyes and was again aware of life and its processes, he had been moved. He did not know it immediately but he had been transferred to The Grandfather's aerie.

The first thing that Comstock was aware of was the fact that he was seated in a chair unlike any he had ever seen before. It was big, and comfortable in a way, except that from the arms of it came metal bands that encompassed his forearms preventing the slightest movement. Around his legs, similar bands held his calves against the legs of the chair.

Directly in front of him was the most tremendous desk he had ever seen. Around the walls of the room, which was completely circular, were little holes, just big enough for the muzzles of stun guns to project through. The portholes were no more than ten inches apart so that every inch of his body was being menaced at all times.

As intelligence returned to him, he looked dully at the too tall figure of The Grandfather who sat behind the desk. The long beard curved gracefully down the giant chest. More tired than he had ever been in his life, Comstock thought in woolly fashion of how nice it would be to curl up in The Grandfather's lap, as he had been taught by his mother, and forget all his cares.

Thinking of The Grandfather's lap made him remember, with a guilty start, that he had no idea of what had happened to Pat.

Before he could ask, The Grandfather said, "You have managed to do something that no one has done in more years than I like to think about. Why did you sneak away from the Boardroom, Comstock?"

The omnipresent muzzles of the circle of stun guns preyed heavily on Comstock's muddled mind. He did not answer the question.

The Grandfather said, "I am not used to having to ask a question twice. Why did you leave when I was speaking? Did you not believe what I was saying?"

There was a curious expression, Comstock realized, on The Grandfather's face. Was it possible that what The Grandfather had said, down below, was not the truth? Could it be that Bowdler was as befuddled as the rest of them? Was some tremendous game, so complicated as not to be understood being played?

"I am waiting," The Grandfather said.

Comstock's slack face betrayed nothing. He was too tired, too confused, too upset to even hazard an opinion. Finally he croaked, "The only reason I left, was because I wanted to think."

"To think?" The tone was satirical. "Curious, most of my people are content to allow *me* to do all the thinking."

How despairingly Comstock wished that he too could let The Grandfather do all his thinking, but it was much too late for that.

Hunching over his desk, The Grandfather leaned forward and said, "Speak up, man, don't force me to employ certain methods which I have used on occasion."

Speak up! When all he wanted to do was lay his weary head on that comforting beard and forget everything? Speak up when his tongue was thick with thirst and his stomach growling with hunger? Speak up when his sleepless head was involuntarily dropping from time to time from sheer fatigue?

Why didn't the old fool leave him alone? How far could a man be pushed? What did he have to lose now that he knew that membership on the Board of Fathers meant a lingering death by heart disease? A wave of adrenaline shot through his system, as anger burned brightly.

He almost snarled as he asked, "Suppose *you* do some answering? Suppose *I* ask the questions for a change?"

Leaning back in his chair The Grandfather's face reflected no emotion at all.

Comstock snapped. "Suppose you tell me how you've stayed in power so long! Some of those earth books I read in Bowdler's library made me wonder about a lot of things, Grandfather. And I'd like to know some of the answers! Tell me, how have you stayed in power so long?"

"Because," The Grandfather said, "since you ask, because of fear."

Of that emotion there was none in Comstock. He was beyond any ordinary feelings at all. They had all been washed away.

CHAPTER FOURTEEN

FEAR?" Comstock hazarded, for at the moment the word meant nothing to him. Nothing at all.

"Fear," The Grandfather said, repeating the word again, "is my bulwark. Cowardice my armor. I am the most frightened man in our world. That is the reason I am The Grandfather. Until the day comes that a more frightened man, a more cowardly human being arises, I shall rule. No brave man can ever breach my defenses, because no brave man can ever know the things I fear. Since I am always fearful my mind is filled with ideas as to where and how I may be attacked. Since this is so, I spend all my waking hours building up my guard against any such attacks.

"The nights," he said thoughtfully, "I spend in nightmares in which all my defenses crumble."

Comstock sat across the room from The Grandfather, his arms enclosed in the cage like affair that immobilized him. Through apertures in the walls at shoulder height he could see the stock-still muzzles of the stun guns that were trained on him. He brought his attention back to The Grandfather. The man's long, thin face was raddled with what seemed like fear. Tics jerked monstrously at the corners of his mouth and at his hag-ridden eyes.

"How," Comstock asked, "can you sit under the menace of the guns that surround us? Aren't you afraid that one of the gunners may shoot you?"

"You see," the lean, bearded face was full of envy, "you think like a brave man and that is why you will never be able to overcome me. Only a brave man could sit under the guns…unless, he had the foresight to have done what I have. Behind the gunners of which you are aware, there is another set of gunners, each of whom has a gun pointed at the head of the gunner who has been honored by being my guard."

Comstock thought of this for a while and then he said, "And do the secondary gunners have tertiary gunners menacing them?"

The Grandfather smiled delightedly. "There! You see, you are beginning to think like a coward. Fear like mine is infectious. Of course there are tertiary and quaternary and quinternary gunners!"

In the lengthening pause that followed this statement of The Grandfather's, Comstock wondered if this was right, was fear the thing that held him on the pinnacle he had made his own?

The Grandfather said, "I am not sure that I have convinced you. Observe my face, the way fear tears at it. Consider that I am so cowardly that my stomach digests itself rather than the food I force into it. Realize that the only pleasure my fear allows me to enjoy is that of power and then try to realize how helpless a brave man like you who spreads his pleasure between the table and the bed must be in the face of my one, all-consuming pleasure.

"You can eat for perhaps three hours a day," The Grandfather went on, "depending on your sexual appetite and your years, you can spend an hour, perhaps two in play at sex. But I can spend every waking minute of every day on my pleasure."

He smiled. "You are helpless, bound by your bravery, you fool!"

And Comstock, considering the matter wondered if The Grandfather was right. One Achilles heel alone remained to attack. Could a coward foresee rashness, foolhardy bravery? Or would a coward be unable to intuitively foresee such an action, to grapple with it; not that he, Comstock, was brave.

Only one other way occurred to Comstock in which the matter could be tested.

Leaning his upper trunk as far forward as his bonds would allow, he said slowly, throwing his words into the teeth of the bearded man who faced him, "You are a liar."

It is an understatement to say that The Grandfather was surprised. His face was absolutely blank as he repeated the word, "Liar?" questioningly.

COMSTOCK was aware in the lengthening silence of the immobility of the single-eyed muzzles of the stun guns, which surrounded him. Not since he had opened his eyes in that singular room had one of the guns so much as twitched.

"Surely," Comstock said. "For instance, there is no one behind any of the guns that seem to menace me."

Lean fingers were busy caressing the silken hairs of the beard that cascaded down The Grandfather's chest. The gaunt face surrounded by the aureole of hair was intent. "How?" he asked, "could you tell that?"

"Because I am *really* a coward." Comstock said almost boldly. "And I know that no coward could really take the chance that an involuntary tightening of a trigger finger, caused, perhaps by a sneeze, could and would mean death. And I know too that it takes courage of a sort to talk about one's own cowardice. For instance, I find this that I am saying very difficult. That little prepared speech you delivered convinced me of only one thing. You are not afraid of anything."

The Grandfather's hand reached out to his desk and his almost too long index finger darted out and pressed a button. Instantly the bonds that had held Comstock immobile in the chair loosened.

The Grandfather said slowly, "Bowdler chose wisely when he selected you as a rebel. Perhaps more wisely even than he knew."

Comstock moved his arms about in the chair, having no desire now that the bonds were no longer holding him, to get to his feet. He was afraid that his wobbling knees would fail to support him. Massaging his arms where the metallic bonds had bitten deep, he waited with some trepidation for what might happen. Whatever it was, he feared it would be highly unpleasant.

It was.

The Grandfather rose from behind the desk and looking down at Comstock from his not inconsiderable height of six feet ten inches, said, "Since, as you have so truly pointed out, the secret of my continued power is not fear, what then, is my secret?"

Comstock had devoted a great deal of cerebration to just this point, but that did not make it any easier to say it aloud.

In the lengthening silence, The Grandfather bent down from his great height till his gaunt, strong face was on a level with Comstock's. "Well?"

"The secret," Comstock said, "is the exact opposite of what you claimed."

"Ahh?" The exclamation was almost jubilant.

"Yes," Comstock hurried on, fearing that if he didn't say it in a rush he never would get out the words. "You don't rule because you are afraid but because there is nothing that you fear."

"Come, come," The Grandfather smiled thinly, "each man, no matter how brave, has some secret fear. For instance fat people fear death."

The change of subject was so sudden that it threw Comstock off his mental stride. "Fat people?" he queried.

"Surely," The Grandfather said, "the thought must have occurred to you. Fat people are fat because they fear dying. Did you ever see a very thin person naked?"

To think, Comstock's veering brain thought, that the day would ever come when he'd hear The Grandfather of all people use a dirty word like n+...d!

"If you've ever seen a thin person nude, you can realize that their skeleton is omnipresent. This, to a fat person, is detestable. They want to hide their ever-present *memento mori* decently. They don't want always to be reminded of that which is hidden inside of all of us, waiting for us... That's why they get fat. Padding. That's all it is, padding to hide the grisly skeleton who sits with us at every feast."

Struggling to get his attention on to this new vagary of The Grandfather, Comstock said, "But fat people die sooner than skinny ones."

"Certainly," The Grandfather nodded, "but what's that got to do with it? That's reality. The statistic that obesity shortens life is hard and true. But that reality only comes once, at the end of the line. To the fat person the important thing to hide from is the ever-present reminder that the day he is born he begins to die. That's the big trick they try to employ. To forget that fact. But I digress. You were saying?"

WHAT had he been saying? This maundering of the Grandfather, could it be that like the Elders, The Grandfather was senile? Comstock looked down at his own beginning paunch and wondered if this was why the Grandfather had brought up the subject of fat, then he said, "I was saying that the reason you rule is because you have no fears."

"Yes. That was the subject under discussion, wasn't it?" Again The Grandfather stroked his beard. "Now then, just how did you arrive at that rather startling idea? Remember I don't agree with you, for as I said, every human being fears something."

"I am sure you are right," Comstock said tensely. "I am sure that every human being fears something...or someone."

"I find your remarks contradictory."

"Not at all," Comstock felt a little bolder. Crossing his arms, he dared the thunderbolts of The Grandfather's wrath. "I don't think you are a human being, grandpa."

The silence that followed his pronouncement seemed to last for all the years of Comstock's life.

When The Grandfather spoke, his words came as a withering shock to Comstock.

"You are a very brave man, Comstock. The bravest this world of ours has produced in five centuries…"

It was, after all, one thing to have an hypothesis, it was an astrobat of a far different color to have that hypothesis substantiated. And right from the astrobat's mouth at that!

Looking down at his hands, Comstock was incuriously aware that they were trembling violently. He brave? The idea was ludicrous. He was more badly scared than he had ever been in his whole life. Fear jumped and jolted his body as he waited for The Grandfather to continue.

"But," The Grandfather said, "I can see that you are on the very brink of nervous exhaustion. I will speak to you more fully when you are fed and rested."

Comstock was too tired to do more than pick at the food that was waiting for him in the bedchamber to which an R.A. guided him. As a matter of fact, seated on the edge of the bed, his head whirling, he was barely aware of Pat's entrance. She had evidently been fed too, for her only concern was Comstock. Going to him, she forced him to lie down, then, as he closed his eyes blissfully at the feeling of ease that welled up in him, she gently spooned food into his mouth till his eyes closed completely.

She slept all that night right next to him, but so deep was his fatigue that it was not till the night that he awoke and by that time Pat had been up and about for hours. She came out of the bath in a swirl of soft cloth. Comstock felt excitement well up in him and knew instantly that he was almost all recovered from the slings and arrows that had assailed him.

Drawing her to him, he was very much aware of her presence this time.

WHEN they had finished making love she said, gently, "I almost forgot, and it's your fault," but her smile proved that she shared the fault if it could be called that, "The Grandfather wants to see you as soon as you rise."

Feeling prepared to tackle legions let alone The Grandfather, Comstock showered, shaved and dressed, whistling all the while. "Any chance of getting some food?" He had yelled through the pouring water so that when he finished dressing, a tray was all set up for him.

Wolfing down the food he listened intently to what Pat had learned during his sleep.

"And the most remarkable thing," Pat said, "is the artificial insemination laboratory downstairs!"

"Wait a minute," Comstock said through a mouthful of food, "what's a laboratory, what's insemination and what's artificial insemination?"

"Bowdler said that the funniest thing that happened when he was trying to make a rebel of you, was when you thought that the Fathers were really the fathers of all the children in the world."

"Wass so funny?" Comstock wanted to know, bread filling his mouth.

"Umm," Pat said. "I better backtrack a bit. As long as the scientists had a hand in running our world they were able to control the birth rate by mechanical means. But when they were killed, The Grandfather was left with the problem of trying to keep our world from being overpopulated without using any mechanics."

Comstock was completely confused but waited patiently, shoveling food into his empty belly while he waited for clarification.

"The first thing that occurred to The Grandfather was to try to control completely the sex drive but...that didn't work very well. Then he reasoned that if the sexual stereotype of women was changed to old women who could no longer bear children that he was then in a position to only have the proper number of women impregnated."

All the obscenity that Pat was mouthing would, a few days ago, have made Comstock faint, or aroused him, but it didn't even occur to him to find it odd.

She continued, "Then as soon as women who were past their menopause had become the love objects, The Grandfather set up a laboratory here in headquarters where the healthiest women in the population could come. Under hypnosis they were injected with live sperm, and lo and behold, the population curve was back under control again!"

Comstock was sure that what Pat was saying was important, but at the moment all he could really think about was his curious duel the night before with The Grandfather.

"With what little scientific gadgets were left after the last scientists were killed, The Grandfather set up a police force, which he called the Father's Right Arms, but not even the R.A.'s know how the radios they use, or the stun guns, or the automobiles that they drive work, let alone knowing about the hypnosis that makes people see haloes around their heads.

"Between his control of the birth rate, his police force, and the little science at his command, he has kept our world running…after a fashion. But the point at which we rebels enter the picture is this."

It was a sure thing that what Pat was saying was vital to her, to him, and to the whole world, but Comstock could not help remembering the outrageous things he had said, and thought about The Grandfather. What could it lead to? Why had the Grandfather called him the most courageous man…

Pat said, "But The Grandfather is only a man and therefore has made mistakes. He has frozen our culture at the same point for so long that humanity is in danger of drying up and dying out."

If, Comstock thought, The Grandfather had been only a man, then all this trouble would not have started, but there was no point in frightening Pat, she was too happy, too bubbling over with excitement, with the news of what a brave new world they were soon to have under the direction of Bowdler, Helen, Grundy, the philosopher, Pat and Comstock.

Comstock wondered vaguely what a philosopher was when Pat mentioned it, but that question too was made meaningless by the things he was worried about.

Leaning forward, Pat kissed Comstock, and said, "Isn't it wonderful, darling? I'm so excited I can hardly sit still." Then, remembering, she said, "But hurry up, sweetheart, you'll have to go see The Grandfather…"

Yes. That was going to be his job.

He had been using it as a device when he had suggested that the Picaroon beard The Grandfather in his lair. But now it was obvious, he, Comstock, was going to have to do precisely that!

CHAPTER FIFTEEN

PAUSING at the door, Comstock turned around to blow a goodbye kiss to Pat. But she had turned with her back to him, which may have been the reason that he at first failed to understand the meaning of what she said to him.

The words, which baffled him were, "Darling, it's all going to be so worth while. It will mean that our child will be born in a world that is worth living in, not this sorry mess through which we have had to struggle."

One hand on the doorknob, one foot raised, about to proceed out through the doorway, Comstock stood stock-still. Then he said, and his voice was quite numb, "Child?"

Turning from the window, Pat smiled and said, "Oh, it's too soon to know, but one of the inevitable results of two people of opposite sexes making love is that a child is born, you know."

"Child?" he repeated.

"Imagine," Pat went on not noticing that her man looked as if he had been pole axed, "our child will be the first love child born for centuries… Isn't that exciting?"

"Child?" he said for the third time and then fainted.

When he came to, Pat said, "I'm sorry, dear, perhaps I shouldn't have mentioned it all so abruptly."

"We're going to have a child. I'll be a father!" Beaming he took her in his arms and kissed her, for the first time the emotion he felt was a completely different kind of love, minus the lustful feelings that being near her generally engendered.

"That is," she said carefully, trying to avoid shocking him again, "we'll have a child if we are successful in what we have been doing."

"It's wonderful fun trying, isn't it?"

"Umm," she said, and kissed him with more fervor.

Neither knew how long the R.A. had been framed in the doorway, his shocked face alternately scarlet and then livid. The man croaked, "The Grandfather awaits your presence, Father Comstock."

Father with a capital F and father with a small f. Now, surely, Comstock thought, he would have the courage to face again the being whom he feared had to be overcome before their desire could come to fruition.

FACING The Grandfather was still difficult, Comstock found. Many things conspired to make it so. First was his training, but second was the terrible ego position of being so much smaller than the towering figure, who stood, beard foaming down his chest, his hands behind his back as he paced back and forth in his sanctum and said, "Just before I feared your imminent collapse last night you said that you did not think I was a human being. Would you care to amplify your statement at this time?"

Rather than stand before The Grandfather, his head tilted back like a child facing an irate parent, Comstock decided to sit down. That way he could stare at The Grandfather's belt and speak to it, instead of getting a crick in his neck.

"Before I go back to that line of thought," Comstock said rather pompously, "I would like to take this opportunity of saying that in some ways I feel you have acted like an egregious idiot."

"Oh?"

"If I understand what I was told, you set up this whole strict very moral world just so that disease could be cured by what our people considered to be sins. Correct?"

"Correct."

"I think you've got the whole thing wrong."

"I see."

"Of course you've been around a lot longer than I have, but if I may say so bold, I think you got the whole blasted thing turned around."

"You are being quite objectionable, Father Comstock."

"Objectionable, perhaps, but I notice that you do not say that I am incorrect in my assumption."

"I am waiting to see what your assumption may be."

"I think that disease is caused by sin."

"And you feel that this is different than saying that sin can cure disease?"

Was the old gent really an imbecile? Comstock wondered irritably. It seemed quite obvious to him that somewhere along the line the basic idea had been lost sight of, and the antithesis set up in its place.

"In one of the earth books I read there was a reference to what was called psychosomatic medicine. Now, if I understood what I read correctly, the theory of this kind of curing was that the person who was sick was punishing himself for some sin that he thought he had committed," Comstock said thoughtfully.

"Yes?"

"The cure then, was to assure the person that his sin was either non-existent or not heinous."

"I see."

"But the way you've run our world, you've made us commit real sins in order to be cured of non-existent diseases."

The Grandfather stared off into space. Then he snapped his fingers and said, "By golly, I bet you're right! Now that you say it out loud that does seem to be what the scientists were thinking about. Guess I got things a little mixed up."

"A little mixed up!" Comstock was incredulous. "You've had us living in a madhouse for five hundred years and all you can say is that you must have made a little mistake?"

Shrugging, The Grandfather said, "So I made a little mistake."

"Now," Comstock said, "now I know that my hypothesis is correct, how could you have listened to the things, the horrors that have gone on in our world for all these centuries and not been affected, not been chilled to the bone with a desire to do something concrete?"

The Grandfather seemed to consider the question carefully, then he shrugged and said, "Who listens?"

There was only one thing that remained for Comstock to do. Marshalling his forces, he suddenly leaped from his chair straight at The Grandfather.

His clutching hands were stretched out in front of him as the forward impetus of his movement carried him into The Grandfather's chest. He pulled at The Grandfather's beard.

Now he would know, once and for all.

And then he knew.

The beard came off in his hands.

CHAPTER SIXTEEN

STUNNED by his own temerity, Comstock stared at what had formerly been hidden by the hair of the beard.

"I knew it." Comstock said at last. "I knew no human being could live for five hundred years."

"That is why I have taunted you into action," The Grandfather said gravely, "I knew that only when you saw with your own eyes the evidence of what you suspected would you be able to proceed properly."

"This is why there is no record of your existence prior to five hundred years ago?"

"Yes."

Staring at the metallic surface that had been hidden under the beard, seeing for the first time the control panel that covered The Grandfather's whole chest, Comstock wondered what to do next.

"I hope," The Grandfather said, "that I have not been derelict to my trust. But somehow the whole thing became too much for the mechanisms that the scientists built into me."

If scientists could do things like this, Comstock thought with a wild surge of hope, if they could have built a thing like this that faced him, that was capable of living for half a thousand years, and had succeeded in behaving like a super-human being, then what other wonders was science capable of bringing about? What would the future hold, released from the dead hands that had held his world in sway for so long? The thought was enough to make his brain spin.

The beard lay across his hands, its very feel a challenge to the imagination for it was not made of hair but some substance unlike any that Comstock had ever seen before.

The Grandfather put his forefinger to a button on the board on his chest. It actuated a servomechanism that allowed him to sit down. He said, "May I have my beard back?"

Witlessly, still astounded at what had come to pass, Comstock handed the object to the man? Thing? That sat across the desk from him.

When The Grandfather was in the act of replacing the beard, Comstock could see just under his chin, a series of rivets that held his head in place. One looked loose and Comstock pointed it out.

The Grandfather tightened the rivet and then sighed. "Yes, there can be no doubt I am beginning to wear out. That is why I have forced this series of actions into being. That is why I forced Bowdler to leave the Board to search for you rebels. I knew that my day was coming to an end.

"I cannot say that I will be sorry to see you go to rust peacefully."

The idea of The Grandfather rusting, so bizarre as to have been unimaginable a few days earlier did not even cause Comstock to flinch.

Forcing himself to listen to what The Grandfather was saying instead of wondering wildly about the future, he heard, "You see it was my primary function to keep the culture frozen till someone, anyone, with intelligence and guts, came along and saw past the facade that had been erected.

"I must confess," The Grandfather said wryly, "that when I first heard about you, I did not think *you* would be the one to tear down that facade."

Since Comstock was as amazed as the robot, he did not find the words insulting. As a matter of fact he was too worried about the next step that had to be taken to think much about what the old machine was saying.

"Shall we join my friends?" Comstock asked and it was only then that he realized how long he had been sitting thinking, for he had not even heard The Grandfather ask for his help.

The machine was frozen in the same position it had assumed when it sat down at the desk. The Grandfather said almost plaintively, "I thought that perhaps you had become deaf."

"Huh?"

"One of my circuits, is jammed. You'll have to help me. This has been happening more and more frequently lately, that's why I was so anxious for assistance."

"What can I do?"

"See if you can rotate the fourth dial on the left, on my chest."

But the dial moved with no result. There was no impulse being sent to motivate the big machine.

LUNATIC thoughts raced through Comstock's now addled brain. He wondered what vice The Grandfather would have to adopt in order to be cured.

"Don't get panicky," The Grandfather said. "It's only my body mechanism that has been affected. In my top desk drawer there is a pair of pliers. Get them."

Obeying, Comstock saw, in the desk drawer next to some tools, a metal memorandum pad. Scrawled on it he read the idea that had held back his world for five centuries. It said, "All or most diseases can be cured, if the very moral people of a very moral civilization are forced to perform actions which they consider immoral." After this statement there were two more words. These, The Grandfather had evidently never considered objectively. The two words were, True? False?

But Comstock did not pause to think about the statement too much. Instead he grabbed the pliers and asked what he was to do with them.

"Unfasten the rivet that holds my head in place," the robot instructed.

Obeying the command was very difficult, Comstock found, for a variety of reasons. First, he had an ingrained feeling that what he was doing was the height of blasphemy, and then, when he controlled this conditioned reflex, he found that time and rust had almost frozen the rivets in place.

He was sweating by the time he had unfastened all the necklace of rivets.

The Grandfather said, "Now, very carefully, lift my head straight upwards."

There were many wires dangling down from the underside of the jaw. The Grandfather directed Comstock to cut them free.

Then and only then, with Comstock holding the head carefully between his blistered hands, The Grandfather said, "Now let us join the others."

IN the Boardroom, The Fathers, Bowdler, the philosopher, Grundy, Pat and Helen sat beneath an inscribed metal plaque, which read:

"Alcoholism cures heart trouble."

"Adultery cures arteriosclerosis."

"Thieving cures insanity."

"Drug addiction cures cancer."

"Prostitution cures diabetes."

There were many such apothegms.

But no one even bothered to read them. As a matter of fact, Grundy had said that one of the first things that they had better do was remove the plaque. The others had agreed heartily.

A loudspeaker above the biggest door in the room said, "The Grandfather approaches."

The Fathers, in a body, forced their decrepit frames to rise.

The rebels decided that they too might as well rise out of respect.

It took a moment before everyone could see the object that Comstock was carrying under his arm.

Walking to the head of the table, Comstock said, "Sit down. Sit down. The Grandfather has a few words to say." Only then did he place the disembodied head he had been carrying onto the table in front of him.

Two of the oldest, sickest Fathers, died immediately.

When their bodies had been removed, Comstock said, "There's nothing to be afraid of. The Grandfather says that He is something that used to be called a robot."

Then rapping on the table with a gavel, he sat back and waited. Down at the far end of the table he could see Pat eyeing the head with awed fascination. The others were equally pop-eyed.

The philosopher, the man of words, could not be restrained. Before the Grandfather could speak, the philosopher asked incredulously, "Do you mean to say that we have been obeying the dictates of a machine?"

Nodding. Comstock said nonchalantly. "Yep."

Then The Grandfather spoke.

"I was made to be your servant, and it has been my sorry task to be your master. I have not enjoyed it and I must say that I am glad at long last to be rid of an onerous task."

Then he went on to describe the way he had tried, in his feeble, mechanical way to do that which he had been ordered to do. When he had finished his apologetic summary, he said, "But time grows ever shorter and I fear that even my carefully made cortex is beginning to go bad. Listen closely for I have no idea when I will cease to function.

"The mistakes I have made, have been errors of commission not omission. When I have failed it was because not even the scientists who made me could foretell what was to be, as no man can.

"I was told, just before the death of the scientist who finished me, that the reason all our people were driven from earth was because they were vestigial hangovers from what he called an inner-directed culture. An inner-directed culture is always the result of an historical period when the death rate is higher than the birth rate. This kind of culture possesses certain attributes which serve pioneers well, because these inner-directed people have a strong sense of right and wrong, they believe implicitly in black and white evils and virtues. But in our world the birth rate is now, because of my machinations, about equal to the death rate, our people live longer, few children are lost at birth, there is enough food to go around, and so it is time to evolve from an inner-directed culture to a more sophisticated one which has been called an other-directed culture.

"Such a culture is hesitant to make value judgments, it can no longer appraise the foibles of other human beings; the righteousness of the inner-directed person gives way to the more adult approach that right and wrong are after all purely subjective concepts.

"These people can be more objective and since they can, they must inevitably be less prone to throw the first stone.

"There are many concomitants of such a culture, but to you will be the wonder and the glory of discovering them. This is your next step.

"Take it wisely."

IT was long before all that The Grandfather said made any sense to his hearers, but all of them remembered the words until the time came that they became understandable.

The last thing that The Grandfather said was, "In the old world from which we came, the earliest known culture was one called an ancestor-directed culture. This was understandable in a period when the death rate was so high and old age rare. Old age became magical since so few possessed it. Then as the elderliness alone ceased to be unique they ascended to the next culture pattern, the one I have described as the inner-directed culture. When your ancestors were sent away from earth almost all the earth people had become other-directed. What has happened in this long hiatus in which we've been out of touch with mother earth I cannot hazard an opinion.

"But if we are to proceed on the previous record we can be sure that they have now ascended to a still higher culture pattern. I would suggest that you not lift the force field that surrounds our planet till you have matured enough to be able to meet your earth cousins on an equal footing.

"An inner-directed culture places a terrific premium on fatherhood. That is why you have been raised with such a high opinion of fathers and why all your power symbols are in terms of fatherhood.

"In the next step which you are to take, fatherhood and motherhood will be equated properly and there will be no further emphasis on what has been called the battle of the sexes.

"The battle of the sexes will become not an armed truce, but an equal sharing of what is best in mankind.

"I have left directions as to how you may contact the interplanetary economy but I suggest you wait till the time is ripe before taking that step.

"And now I am about to go out of phase. At last...at long last...I thought it would never come..."

The eyes closed and the robot was still.

It never spoke again.

Pat ran to Comstock's side. His waiting arms engulfed her as they stood, looking deeply into each other's eyes, savoring their moment of triumph, and thinking with delight of what the future held.

Comstock said, "I love you."

It was the first time in five hundred years that the air of that planet had heard those words said in a tone that meant by love—sharing and trust and hope and peace, and mutual sacrifice that something bigger and better might come from that love.

THE END

If you've enjoyed this book, you will not want to miss these terrific titles...

ARMCHAIR SCI-FI, FANTASY, & HORROR DOUBLE NOVELS, $12.95 *each*

D-1   **THE GALAXY RAIDERS** by William P. McGivern
          SPACE STATION #1 by Frank Belknap Long

D-2   **THE PROGRAMMED PEOPLE** by Jack Sharkey
          SLAVES OF THE CRYSTAL BRAIN by William Carter Sawtelle

D-3   **YOU'RE ALL ALONE** by Fritz Leiber
          THE LIQUID MAN by Bernard C. Gilford

D-4   **CITADEL OF THE STAR LORDS** by Edmund Hamilton
          VOYAGE TO ETERNITY by Milton Lesser

D-5   **IRON MEN OF VENUS** by Don Wilcox
          THE MAN WITH ABSOLUTE MOTION by Noel Loomis

D-6   **WHO SOWS THE WIND...** by Rog Phillips
          THE PUZZLE PLANET by Robert A. W. Lowndes

D-7   **PLANET OF DREAD** by Murray Leinster
          TWICE UPON A TIME by Charles L. Fontenay

D-8   **THE TERROR OUT OF SPACE** by Dwight V. Swain
          QUEST OF THE GOLDEN APE by Ivar Jorgensen and Adam Chase

D-9   **SECRET OF MARRACOTT DEEP** by Henry Slesar
          PAWN OF THE BLACK FLEET by Mark Clifton.

D-10   **BEYOND THE RINGS OF SATURN** by Robert Moore Williams
          A MAN OBSESSED by Alan E. Nourse

ARMCHAIR SCIENCE FICTION CLASSICS, $12.95 each

C-1   **THE GREEN MAN**
          by Harold M. Sherman

C-2   **A TRACE OF MEMORY**
          By Keith Laumer

C-3   **INTO PLUTONIAN DEPTHS**
          by Stanton A. Coblentz

ARMCHAIR MASTERS OF SCIENCE FICTION SERIES, $16.95 each

M-1   **MASTERS OF SCIENCE FICTION, Vol. One**
          Bryce Walton—"Dark of the Moon" and other tales

M-2   **MASTERS OF SCIENCE FICTION, Vol. Two**
          Jerome Bixby: "One Way Street" and other tales

If you've enjoyed this book, you will not want to miss these terrific titles...

ARMCHAIR SCI-FI & HORROR DOUBLE NOVELS, $12.95 each

D-11   **PERIL OF THE STARMEN** by Kris Neville
THE STRANGE INVASION by Murray Leinster

D-12   **THE STAR LORD** by Boyd Ellanby
CAPTIVES OF THE FLAME by Samuel R. Delaney

D-13   **MEN OF THE MORNING STAR** by Edmund Hamilton
PLANET FOR PLUNDER by Hal Clement and Sam Merwin, Jr.

D-14   **ICE CITY OF THE GORGON** by Chester S. Geier and Richard Shaver
WHEN THE WORLD TOTTERED by Lester Del Rey

D-15   **WORLDS WITHOUT END** by Clifford D. Simak
THE LAVENDER VINE OF DEATH by Don Wilcox

D-16   **SHADOW ON THE MOON** by Joe Gibson
ARMAGEDDON EARTH by Geoff St. Reynard

D-17   **THE GIRL WHO LOVED DEATH** by Paul W. Fairman
SLAVE PLANET by Laurence M. Janifer

D-18   **SECOND CHANCE** by J. F. Bone
MISSION TO A DISTANT STAR by Frank Belknap Long

D-19   **THE SYNDIC** by C. M. Kornbluth
FLIGHT TO FOREVER by Poul Anderson

D-20   **SOMEWHERE I'LL FIND YOU** by Milton Lesser
THE TIME ARMADA by Fox B. Holden

ARMCHAIR SCIENCE FICTION CLASSICS, $12.95 each

C-4   **CORPUS EARTHLING**
by Louis Charbonneau

C-5   **THE TIME DISSOLVER**
by Jerry Sohl

C-6   **WEST OF THE SUN**
by Edgar Pangborn

ARMCHAIR SCIENCE FICTION & HORROR GEMS SERIES, $12.95 each

G-1   **SCIENCE FICTION GEMS, Vol. One**
Isaac Asimov and others

G-2   **HORROR GEMS, Vol. One**
Carl Jacobi and others